DIED

in the

WOOL

DIED
in the
WOOL

A Massachusetts Mayhem Mystery

Elizabeth Ludwig and Janelle Mowery

BARBOUR
PUBLISHING

ISBN 978-1-60260-337-0

Scripture taken from the HOLY BIBLE, NEW INTERNATIONAL VERSION ®. NIV ®. Copyright © 1973, 1978, 1984 by International Bible Society. Used by permission of Zondervan. All rights reserved.

This book is a work of fiction. Names, characters, places, and incidents are either products of the author's imagination or used fictitiously. Any similarity to actual people, organizations, and/or events is purely coincidental.

Cover design: Faceout Studio, www.faceoutstudio.com

Published by Barbour Publishing, Inc., P.O. Box 719, Uhrichsville, Ohio 44683, www.barbourbooks.com

Our mission is to publish and distribute inspirational products offering exceptional value and biblical encouragement to the masses.

Member of the
Evangelical Christian
Publishers Association

Printed in the United States of America.

Dedication

To our Lord Jesus Christ

Acknowledgments: We would like to thank our family and friends for helping make this book possible. Your willingness to read and share in the excitement is what encouraged us to keep writing.

To our critique partners, Jessica Dotta, Jessica Ferguson, Michelle Griep, Marcia Gruver, Gina Holmes, Ane Mulligan, Sandra Robbins, and Susan Sleeman, thank you! You made our work shine.

A special thanks to Lt. John Shauberger and Shane Stensland for their expertise and patience in answering our questions.

And to our dear husbands, thank you for your patience and support. Your belief inspired us, your steadfast commitment anchored us, and your love protected us from the storms of rejection and enabled us to see this day.

CHAPTER ONE

Colder than a murdering mortician's morgue.

No, wait. Librarian Monah Trenary mentally crossed out the line and tried again. *Colder than a murderous mortician's morgue.* She scratched her head and bit her lip. Were morgues cold? She'd only been in the local mortuary once, but it didn't seem nearly as chilly as the library today. Much colder and she wouldn't be able to control the chattering of her teeth.

She flipped her long, dark hair over her shoulder and cast a glance toward the back room. What was taking that air conditioning guy so long anyway? He'd been working at least an hour. Surely he could shut the whole unit down until he fixed it so she could thaw out.

The cold had already chased several patrons away this morning. Monah had to send her teenage assistant, Jamie Canon, out for a couple of space heaters just to keep the rest from leaving. Well, except for Dena Drolen. Her habit of coming in to see if her mail had ended up here by mistake proved to be almost as bothersome as when Monah had to take it to her. Especially when she made Monah run around the library collecting information about one thing or another. Last week, it was engineering and car parts. Today, legal guides and medical journals. The woman couldn't have left soon enough as far as Monah was concerned. She'd have to try again to straighten out the workers at the post office.

The front door whooshed open, and her assistant, Sandy Magrew, rushed in. Older than Monah by almost thirty years, Sandy felt more like a matronly friend than a co-worker. She peered around the room and skittered to a stop across the counter from Monah.

"Good. You're alone." She leaned close and lowered her voice. "You'll never guess who I saw at lunch today."

Monah crumpled the paper she'd been writing on and tossed it atop the full trash can. "Who?"

An excited shiver shook Sandy's ample frame. "Wayne Drolen. Thankfully he didn't see me, so I could eavesdrop on what he was saying." She peeked over her glasses and sucked air through her teeth—her usual attempt to appear ashamed. One corner of her mouth rose. "It didn't hurt that I ducked a little lower in the booth. Was that wrong?"

Monah bit the inside of her cheek. She knew better than to listen to gossip, but wondering who he spoke to didn't count as gossip, did it? Besides, the battle for the funds donated to the city kept getting more and more intense, and Wayne was her biggest opponent. The library, woefully behind the times, needed new computers, and she needed to learn something—anything—to keep the playing field level. "Who was he talking to?"

"His fishing buddy, Gary Walker."

"Oh." Pressing her lips together to keep from asking, Monah silently willed Sandy to continue.

The two stared at each other, waiting for the other's prompting. Sandy broke first.

"All right, I'll just tell ya. . .since I know you wanna know."

The whole top half of her body now lay on the counter. "Wayne told Gary he hired a publicist to help him sell the community on a sports complex. Said a little help on the side wouldn't hurt his odds. Even said she was easy on the eyes." She stood upright and straightened her blouse. "What a weasel."

"A publicist, huh?" Monah's heart thumped.

"Yep. Sounds like he intends to get every dime of that money, dear." Sandy patted her hand. "Hate to say it, but you'd better get on the ball if you want even a fraction."

Voices at the front door silenced them. Several teenagers paraded in, followed by a dour Miss Tait. The teacher's attempts to shush them fell on deaf ears.

Sandy scooped an armful of books off the counter. "Here comes another one of the money grabbers. Don't you worry, Monah. I intend to do whatever I can to make sure the library gets its share."

A snarl lifted the corner of Sandy's lips, and Monah groaned in understanding. "Why doesn't Miss Tait call and tell me when she's going to cart her summer school students in here?"

Air hissed through Sandy's teeth. "Oh, I'm sorry, dear. She did call. Said she borrowed the school van so the kids could all get their reports done at once. Guess I forgot to tell you." She hustled around the counter. "I'm going to the office. Too much work to do to deal with the likes of—"

The last word was lost in the slamming of the office door. *Chicken.* Monah grimaced, wishing she could follow Sandy and avoid the commotion this group always caused.

"Hey, Miss Trenary," the teens chimed as they filed past.

"Remember," Miss Tait called out, waving three of her bony fingers in the air, "I want three references for the author you choose. You're free to leave once your report is in my possession."

She turned to Monah and scowled. "Yet another misuse of city funds, eh, Miss Trenary? You've no cause to have it so cold in here. It may be warmer outside than a usual Massachusetts summer, but this is ridiculous. I'll be sure to let the city council know about your disregard for proper money management."

"There's something wrong with the air conditioner. The repairman is working on it." Monah hated the defensive tone in her voice.

"Yes, well, don't think I won't hold you responsible if I catch my death in here."

Oh, please. "Here. Take my sweater." She pulled it free from the back of her chair and handed it across the counter. "It'll help until the repairman is finished."

The old teacher snatched it from her grasp and stalked away, her heavy heels clomping despite the carpeted floor. *Is it me or all humans in general?* The woman didn't seem to like anyone.

"Miss Trenary, where can I find books about—?"

She didn't hear the rest of Ashley Knight's question. She knew this would happen. With only one reference computer, the students would bombard her with questions about where to find what they wanted.

"The school system is in far too dire a need of funds," Miss Tait once said, "to be thinking about turning the library into an Internet café."

Oh well. Maybe one day Miss Tait would understand the need. In the meantime, Monah wouldn't let the grouchy teacher spoil the day. Besides, she enjoyed every aspect of the library and hoped to teach that love to the kids.

"What is it you're looking for, Ashley?"

Relief washed across the girl's face. "We're supposed to pick a famous author from the old days and write a report. I need three books about whomever I pick."

Monah fought a smile at her "old days" comment. What did Ashley consider old? Then again, maybe she didn't want to know. "And who did you decide on?"

The girl lifted a shoulder. "I don't know. You got any suggestions?"

Monah peeked down a long aisle to see if Miss Tait could see them. The old woman's head was bowed, her fingers riffling through the pages of a book. Monah pulled her gaze back to Ashley. "Well, Samuel Clemens would be an easy one. Or you could write about Nathaniel Hawthorne or Ralph Waldo Emerson. Then there's Longfellow or Edgar Allan Poe. If you want a female to write about, there's Harriet Beecher Stowe and Laura Ingalls Wild. . .er." She drifted into silence at Ashley's openmouthed stare.

"How do you know all that stuff?"

She feigned insulted astonishment and put her hands on her hips. "Hey, I know stuff."

Ashley held her hands out. "No. I only meant—"

With a laugh, Monah slipped her arm around the girl and led her toward the biographies. "I knew what you meant. Just choose someone, and I'll show you the books you can use."

"See, that's what I mean. How do you know where to find that stuff? There's tons of books in here."

She stopped to look Ashley in the eye. "I've worked here for a while. Everything's been laid out the same way for years. For instance, all the biographies are in the 900 section along this wall." She motioned to the number. "And there's more about American authors in the 800s. Plus, I love books. I love the way they feel. I even love their scent." She pulled one off the shelf. "Here, smell."

Ashley took a big whiff. Monah saw the sneeze coming and felt in her pockets for a tissue, but she was too late. Ashley didn't just sneeze, not the expected dainty "a-choo." She exploded with a manly blast. So much for a quiet library.

"Sorry, Ashley. Guess I should have checked for dust. Though"—she looked around—"I think you took care of that little problem for me."

The girl giggled, her palm rubbing at her nose.

"Miss Trenary!"

Miss Tait scowled at them from the end of the aisle. Monah turned back to Ashley and made a face. "You got me into trouble," she whispered with a grin then raised her voice. "You should find what you're looking for in this area, Ashley. Let me know if you need help."

Miss Tait's stare burned into her back all the way to the counter. More visitors had arrived and cluttered the aisles, among them a couple of her regulars, Robin Beck and her daughter, Lauren. The others probably just wanted to get in from the heat. Not Robin. Lauren, a graduate student from the university, hoped to be a teacher and loved spending time in the library. Monah gave her a quick wave.

Miss Tait's sharp gaze still followed her as Monah scanned returned books and prepared to replace them on the shelves. Sunlight sparkled off the leaded glass of the front door as Detective Mike Brockman walked in. Back when Monah's friend Casey Alexander refused to believe her aunt had committed suicide, Mike had been the only officer in the Pine Mills Police Department determined to track down the real killer. His smile was the balm on her otherwise unpleasant day. It also sent Monah's pulse into hyperdrive. She shoved her glasses higher on her nose until her lashes bumped against the lenses. A raise of her eyebrows dropped them back into place. *Think before you speak so you don't make a fool of yourself.* She met him at the front desk.

"Hey, Monah."

"Hi, Mike."

He smiled, his brown eyes twinkling. "You've got it plenty cool in here."

"Yeah. The air is stuck in the ON position. I've got Jimmy checking it, but maybe I should check on him. He's been at it for quite a while now, and I haven't seen a thing of him. He probably decided to take a nap. I heard someone caught him doing that on the job." *Time to shut up, Monah.* She clamped her mouth closed.

Mike leaned his forearms on the counter, his face only inches from hers, his woodsy aftershave tickling her nose. "Yeah, well, I don't know that you should believe everything you hear. People in this town like to talk."

Drawn by his quiet voice and mesmerizing brown eyes, she rested her hip against the counter, bringing her that much closer to him. "You're right. My mistake." She had to get a handle on her reaction to this guy.

He grinned. "You—"

The glass on the front door sparkled again. *Now what?*

Ken Greer, the town's fire chief, thumped the counter as he approached.

"Hello, Monah. Inspection day. I'll be doing the usual checks." He slapped Mike on the back. "Hey, Mike. Everything okay?"

They shook hands. "Sure is. Just here to give Monah a message."

"Riiight."

Monah caught Ken's wink and shrank in dismay, yet a tiny thrill went through her at the thought that maybe the two of them had been talking.

"All right, I'm going to work," Ken said. "Shouldn't take more than an hour or so. Any problems I should know about?"

Monah shuddered and rubbed her arms. "You mean other than an air conditioner that won't turn off? No."

"It is a bit chilly in here. Jimmy working on it?" When she nodded, he knocked on the counter two more times. "Well, if he's not finished by the time I am, I'll go see if I can give him a hand."

As soon as the words left his mouth, the air conditioner fell silent. Monah couldn't help but grin. "Not a moment too soon. I was ready to prop open the front doors."

Ken gave a wave over his shoulder as he headed toward the back. She turned to Mike.

"You said you had a message for me?"

"Yes, but you're not going to like it much, I'm afraid."

Monah's fingers tightened around the spine of a book. *He's going to back out of our double date with Luke and Casey.*

"I won't make the movie tonight. The boss wants me to stake out a warehouse and see if I can catch whoever's burning the abandoned buildings around town."

She wanted to stick out her lower lip as far as it would go in a big pout. She wanted to rant and rave. "You can't order an officer to do that?"

He smiled and touched her chin with his thumb. "I wish. He specifically said me. I'm sorry, Monah. I was looking forward to a little time with you."

"Well, maybe we—"

"Hey, Monah." Jimmy skirted the counter and sat on her stool.

Drat. Now he decides to show up. She managed a tight smile. "Get it fixed?"

"I think so." He spun around on the stool like a little kid. "You had some weird corrosion on your wires. Don't know what caused it, but I think you're good to go now."

Round and round the carrottopped head went. The spinning had to stop. He was making her dizzy. She put out her hand and grabbed his shoulder. "Do you have a bill for me?"

"Nope. Our secretary will send it." He scooted off the stool and headed for the door, his pants hanging low. "Let me know if you still have problems," he said as he strolled out the door.

Mike chuckled. "He's never in a big hurry, is he?"

"I know, and it drives his dad crazy. He's even threatened to dissolve the partnership. But Jimmy's good at what he does, so it's an idle threat."

"Yeah. Anyway, about tonight—"

"Monah, I can't seem to find the latest Brandy Purcell mystery. Is it out yet?" Looking much like the tiny bird she was named after, Robin Beck, her head tilted slightly, peered around a bookshelf at Monah.

She gave an inward groan. Didn't Robin know better than to interrupt a conversation between a potential married couple? Well, okay, so maybe she was jumping the gun on the marriage thing, but a girl could dream, couldn't she?

Mike tapped the counter. "I gotta run. Call you later."

"Oh, okay." She waved, but her heart dropped to her painted toenails. After a moment, she turned to Robin. "It comes out next month, Robin. I'll let you know when I get it in."

"All right. Thanks, Monah." She held up a brightly colored novel, the title spelled in jagged letters across the cover. "I just love these books. I learn as much from them as I do those crime-scene shows."

Monah smiled, nodded, and watched through the window as Mike drove away. "Yeah, me, too." By the time she turned back, Robin had wandered off, only to be replaced by Miss Tait. Wonderful.

"Here's your sweater back." She shoved it toward Monah. "I'm plenty warm now."

She did look a little hot, with flushed cheeks and her hair sticking to her sweaty brow. Monah placed a light touch to her elbow. "Do you feel okay? Would you like some water?"

Miss Tait pressed a shaky palm to her face. "That does sound good. Is it cold?"

She looked for the case of bottled water under the counter. "No, it's just room temperature. I'm sorry." Where'd the water go? "Hang on a minute. I have to ask Sandy where she moved it. In fact, why don't you go on back to your table? I'll bring it to you."

"Thank you."

Monah's brows rose as Miss Tait walked away. Wow. That had to be the nicest the old teacher had ever been to her. She shook her head and went to the office.

"Sandy, where's the bottled water? Miss Tait needs one. I had them under the counter."

"I know. I thought they looked tacky there, so I moved them." She pulled one out from under the desk.

"When did you do that?"

"Just a little while ago. I wanted one, too."

"Okay, thanks." She took the bottle and left the office. Before she could talk to Miss Tait, one of the teens popped into her path. Young Mr. Paul Dyer was a demanding soul, fueled by the fact that his father chaired the school board. It also didn't hurt that they were rich. She set the bottle on Miss Tait's table next to a small pile of reports and crossed her arms.

Out of the corner of her eye, she saw Jamie return with the space heaters. It was about time. The girl waved and mouthed an apology. Monah's attention went back to the student. "What can I do for you, Paul?"

He speared a glance at Miss Tait. "I need one more reference for my author, and I can't find one. I've got to get a good grade on this report, or I won't get an A."

Monah grabbed his arm and pulled him toward the shelves. "Keep your voice down. You may have wanted Miss Tait to hear you, but no one else needs to be in on your grumbling."

"Sorry."

Right. He didn't look a bit sorry, what with the smirk and glance over his shoulder at the old teacher. Monah took a deep breath. "Who's the author?"

"William Faulkner."

Oh, what she wouldn't give for computers. He'd be able to find more information about Faulkner on the Web than in the library. Now that she thought about it, she wouldn't mind some additional funds for more books, too. She pointed. "Try that one."

"I used that one already."

She moved down.

"How about—"

"That one, too."

Grrrr. Okay, she knew one he wouldn't know about. "Here." She pulled out a large tome. "This one is filled with American authors."

"Oh. Great." He took it and turned without so much as a thank-you.

She peeked at her watch. Casey would be dropping by soon, and they would meet with Luke. They had made plans for dinner and a movie, but there was still more than an hour and a half before she could close up. Right now, that felt like forever.

A masculine voice called her name. She gritted her teeth and turned. Mr. Dyer had entered the library and stood looking down at her.

"My son finished yet? I'd like to get home."

Wouldn't we all. Monah forced a smile. "I'm not sure. You can ask Miss Tait, since she gave him the assignment." She motioned to the teacher going over some papers at the table. One corner of Mr. Dyer's mouth tightened, a sure sign he didn't relish the confrontation, but he headed toward her anyway. Jerking out a chair, he sat down next to Miss Tait. To Monah's surprise, the two skipped right past any pleasant greetings, and before long, it appeared they were quarreling. Finally, Mr. Dyer pulled a billfold from the pocket of his jacket, took out a couple of bills, and pushed them toward Miss Tait. Monah leaned closer.

"Pssst."

Monah jumped back. Casey stood at the end of the aisle, a smile pasted on her face. She was early, but Monah didn't mind. Her friend was a welcome distraction from this long day. The two wandered back to the front desk. Several patrons had left. Others, like Robin, seemed intent on staying till closing. She sat at a table with a magazine in her hand.

"You look a little frayed around the edges. Rough day?"

Leave it to Casey to lay it out as she saw it. Monah only hoped she hadn't looked too frayed when Mike stopped by earlier. Casey, on the other hand, always looked great. Her blond hair cascaded over her shoulders and flipped out at just the right angle. Added to that, the blue of her cotton sundress accentuated her eyes. Monah sighed. "You could say that. I'm ready for a relaxing meal and a movie. Where's Luke?"

"He said to call him when we picked a place to eat."

"Okay." Her lips dipped into a frown. "You know our night out will be without Mike."

"I know. He called Luke." Casey gave her a grimacing smile. "How'd you take the news?"

"About like you would if Luke backed out on you."

"That bad, huh?"

The two shared a grin right up until Ken set up his ladder with a clatter that had all the patrons turning heads. He scrambled up the rungs and reached for the sprinklers. Monah rushed to his side.

"Why can't you call me and set up an appointment to do this? The noise is causing too much of a disturbance."

"You know the answer to that, Monah. A surprise inspection isn't a surprise when I make an appointment." He grinned at his own joke. "Hey, do you mind holding the bottom of the ladder for me? You wouldn't want me to fall and cause a disturbance."

Monah looked at Casey and rolled her eyes. Her friend smiled and motioned that she was going into the office. Monah nodded and turned her attention back to Ken.

"Are you going to have to check every single sprinkler in here?" She glanced at her watch and then grabbed hold of the ladder.

"I'll have you out of here by closing time. Promise."

For the next hour, Sandy watched the counter while Monah helped Ken move around the building.

"Everything looks good, Monah. I'm going to check the fire extinguisher in the back, and then I'll be out of your way till the next time."

"Great." Monah slid onto her stool, propped her elbows on the counter, and dropped her face into her palms. What a day. Right now, a movie didn't sound like much fun. At this rate, she'd fall asleep during the previews. She stifled a yawn and looked around. The place was empty. When did that happen?

Casey, Jamie, and Sandy came out of the office.

Sandy set a paperback on the counter next to her purse. "We're headed home, dear. Anything you want us to do before we leave?"

"No thanks. It appears we're done. Sorry I wasn't at the counter much."

"Not a problem. I only checked out two books all afternoon." Sandy waggled her fingers. " 'Bye, girls. Have a nice evening."

Ken scurried from the back and grabbed his ladder. "Hey, Miss Magrew, Jamie. Would you two mind holding that door for me?"

Once they were gone, Monah closed her eyes and clasped Casey's hand. "Listen." She loved it.

"What?"

"Don't you hear that?"

After a moment, Casey shook her head. "No. What?"

"It's quiet."

Casey swatted her on the arm. "Libraries are supposed to be quiet."

"You'd think, huh? Today was anything but. From Ashley's booming sneezes to Ken and his ladder."

Monah walked around the counter and flipped off all the light switches. Only the shimmer of the Exit sign above the door remained. "You ready?"

"You know it. Where do you want to eat?"

"I thought maybe—"

A soft glow lit the back of the library. She headed that way. "Hang on. Ken must have left a light on."

The corridor to the bathroom stretched out black and uninviting. Behind her, bookshelves loomed high overhead like eerie sentinels. The library sure could be creepy after closing. Her steps slowed, and the hair on her neck stood on end. "Anybody back here?"

"Monah?" Casey called from the front.

"Coming." Monah halted outside the restroom. Light spilled

under the door and shone on her toes. She hesitated to push it open. "H–hello? Is anyone in there?"

No answer.

"Good grief. This is silly." She shoved on the door and stepped inside.

Two hose-clad legs protruded from under the stall. Monah stumbled and caught herself on the bathroom sink.

"Oh!" She slapped her hand to her chest to calm the frightened beating of her heart. Finally, she inched forward, just enough to poke at the stall door with her finger. It swung open wide. "Ma'am? Are you. . . ?"

Monah's stomach lurched. A scream clawed at her throat. Sprawled on the floor, her head tilted oddly against the porcelain commode, lay Miss Tait.

"Casey!" The name came out in a squeal. "Call an ambulance!"

CHAPTER TWO

Squad cars blocked the driveway when Mike screeched up to the library. His hands tightened on the steering wheel, and a bead of sweat rolled down the back of his neck. He'd gotten here as fast as he could, but already yellow police tape fluttered from the entrance.

Hunched in front of the two-story brick building sat an ambulance, its back doors swung wide to receive. . .who? The call that came just as he got to Bingham's abandoned warehouse said "unidentified body." His gut tensed as he climbed from the car and slammed the door. Where was Monah?

"Detective Brockman, I'm glad you're here." Wilson Parker, the officer recently transferred from the Boston Police Department, hurried over, his face red and eyes bright. "I've secured the area, sir, and I'm compiling a list of witnesses."

Mike held up his hand. "Back up. Tell me what happened."

"Unattended death. According to her driver's license, the victim is one Charlotte Tait, female, sixty-two years old. We found her in the ladies' restroom, a nasty gash on the back of her head. I'm no medical examiner, but it looks to me like she's been dead at least an hour, maybe two." Parker hooked his thumbs inside his belt. "I'd say we have a murder case on our hands."

"Parker—" Mike took a breath and forced himself to calm

down. Parker was excited, anxious to prove himself, that was all. "Where's the JP?"

"Inside." Parker jerked his head toward the library. "You want me to question the suspects while you look for him?"

"What suspects?"

"The librarian and her friend."

Monah and Casey. Mike tamped his anger and shook his head. "I can handle it."

Parker dropped his hands from his belt to his sides. "But, sir, what if they're in this together? You may want to question them individually. While you're working on one, I'll soften up the other."

Mike sighed. "This isn't Boston. Did it ever occur to you that maybe Miss Tait died of natural causes?"

Parker's owl-like eyes widened. "Huh?"

"You said her driver's license showed she was sixty-two. How do you know she didn't have a heart condition or liver disease or an aneurysm? She could have died from food poisoning. Did you think of that?"

"But the cut on her head—"

"Could have happened when she fell."

Disappointment bent Parker's shoulders. "Oh."

"Cheer up. Maybe somebody will get murdered next week."

Parker brightened. "You think so?"

"No, I don't." Somehow, Mike managed to keep a straight face. "Where is Mon—Miss Trenary?"

"With Officer Crowley."

Mike strode across the library parking lot. Monah and Casey sat huddled together in the backseat of Crowley's squad car. The young teen Monah hired to work summers perched on the hood, her teeth giving her nails a workout.

"Monah?" Her head lifted. Behind her black-rimmed glasses, her brown eyes filled with tears. Mike's heart jerked. "Are you okay?"

She scrambled out of the car. "I'm. . .I. . .did they tell you?"

"About Miss Tait?" He nodded and resisted the urge to pull her into a hug. "Yeah." His glance transferred to Casey, who followed Monah more slowly out of the car. "Who found her?"

Casey tipped her head toward Monah.

"I did."

The tremor in her voice proved his undoing. He reached for her. "Monah—"

"Detective Brockman?" Bill Stackhouse had been the justice of the peace in Pine Mills for as long as Mike could remember. Shorter than Mike by a head, he burst from the library doors like a minilocomotive, his thick legs churning. Across his black windbreaker, the words JUSTICE OF THE PEACE were emblazoned in bright yellow letters. "Could I have a word?"

Mike shot a glance at Monah. "Wait here, okay?"

For once speechless, she bit her lip and nodded.

Mike whirled and took the library's marbled steps two at a time. The door held wide, Bill moved aside to allow Mike to enter then led him toward the restrooms. They ducked under the police tape stretched across the door and went inside.

Mike cast a quick glance around the lavatory. Dated by the brass fixtures and antique lighting, it was the last place he would have pictured finding a body. "Whatcha got?"

"I'm ordering an autopsy since the victim was unattended at the time of death. It's standard procedure but probably unnecessary. From the initial statements Parker collected, Miss Tait appeared pale, sweaty, even complained to that teen sitting on the hood of Officer Crowley's car about chest pain and dizziness."

He pointed toward the commode. "It looks like she got sick, too. We found vomit on the toilet rim and floor. My guess is, it'll be pretty cut-and-dried. Heart attack."

"Okay."

"In the meantime, I'm going to order the library sealed. Got a man you can post outside until we've canvassed the place?"

Mike nodded. "Parker."

"Good." Bill glanced at the woman lying on the floor and shook his head. "Sad. Monah said she's got a sister and niece living in Foxboro. Can you take care of notifying them?"

Mike made a mental note to ask Monah for the number. "Okay. Do we have photos of the body?"

"Done. The crime-scene unit took care of it before you got here. We've got fingerprints and specimen samples, too. I'll get one of them to take care of her belongings. After that, we'll be ready for the ambulance crew."

"I'll let them know." He glanced at the sheet-draped figure on the floor and said a quick prayer for her family. Even somebody as grouchy as Miss Tait had people who loved her, and he dreaded that he'd have to give them the news she was gone. With a shake of his head, he ducked back under the tape line and went to find Monah.

~

Ambulance attendants wheeled the body out of the library. Bill held one door and Mike, the other. Monah watched, wanting to reach out to Miss Tait, help her in some way, but it was too late. The woman who'd rendered such a giant presence in life looked so tiny under the white sheet.

A group of people clustered on the sidewalk. Others tried to see what was happening from the street. Irritation flared in Monah's chest. Gawkers. Why didn't they go home?

Just as quickly as her anger surged, it faded to a dull pang. She might very likely have done the same had it occurred anywhere else. She scanned the faces, meeting the gaze of many. Some were sympathetic and kind. Others seemed downright accusatory, as if she held some of the blame for whatever illness took Miss Tait.

The familiar feeling of being judged crept over her. She closed her eyes for a moment. That was ridiculous, and she wouldn't let herself fall into that trap again. Sensitivity to what people thought hounded her more than she liked to admit.

A car, followed closely by a van, screeched to a halt next to the ambulance. Monah recognized the local radio and newspaper teams rushing toward Mike, no doubt in a race to be first to get the information out to the public. She couldn't fault the morbid curiosity of people. They were human. Thankfully, Mike ushered the crews back.

Ken Greer showed up just as the ambulance pulled away. He jumped out of his truck and wove his way past the throng to Mike's side. "I heard the news when I got back to the station. Can I help?"

"Yeah. See if you can get this crowd to dissipate. There's nothing to see here." Mike spoke loudly enough for everyone to hear. His announcement was met with several moans and grumbles.

Ken nodded. "Come on, everyone. You heard the detective." He used gentle pushes to get the group moving. "Go on home." Parker followed his lead and helped in the attempt to send the crowd on their way.

While Ken and the officer dealt with the onlookers, Mike fended off the media, telling them they'd know something when he did, but they continued to dog his footsteps. After one last look around, Monah turned and stared at the bricked facade of the Pine Mills Public Library. The last rays of evening sun glanced off the windows. Blues and purples flushed the sky above the corniced eaves. Attendance tomorrow would more than likely surge. People would be disappointed to discover there was nothing more she could tell them. Maybe the furor would die down in a hurry.

"You okay?" Casey touched her shoulder and dipped her head to peer into Monah's face.

Monah shot a quick glance at Jamie. Seated on the hood of the car, popping her gum, the girl appeared oblivious. Monah shrugged. "Yeah. I'm just not looking forward to all the questions from patrons tomorrow. You know this town. The gossip will go on until every last detail is discovered and mulled over too many times." She sighed. "It seems disrespectful."

Casey nodded. "I know. I went through the same feelings when Aunt Liddy disappeared back in April." The two shared a hug. "It won't last long. They'll forget the moment the next gossip-worthy event takes place."

Monah ran her hand over her heated face. "I don't think I'll ever be able to forget the sight of Miss Tait's body on the floor. It was awful."

"Monah?" Mike strode toward her, Parker right behind. "How're you doing?"

His eyes told her everything he couldn't say in front of the officer. She nodded. Maybe they'd get some time to talk in private later.

"I need to get a statement from you, Casey, and—" He glanced at Jamie, uncertainty in his gaze.

Monah prodded his memory. "Jamie Canon."

The officer at Mike's side nearly vibrated with excitement. "I'll take the statements if you like, Detective."

"Parker." Strain coarsened Mike's voice. "Go guard the door or something." He waited for the officer to leave then shook his head. "I hope I didn't act like that when I was a rookie. I'd hate to think I got under my superior's skin trying for a promotion."

Monah slipped her arms around her middle. Mike would never do that. He was too humble and considerate.

"So, tell me what happened." Mike touched her arm softly. "Monah, you go first."

She repeated the same story she'd told the justice of the peace.

"You didn't move her, right?" Mike raised his eyebrows.

"No. I only touched her leg when I called her name."

"Okay." He pulled a spiral notebook from his pocket, made a notation, then looked at her again, all business. "Bill told me you said something about Miss Tait appearing sick?"

"Oh yes. Earlier this afternoon, she looked a little sweaty and her complexion was—I don't know—pasty, I guess. I offered her some water, and she took it."

Mike wrote that down. "That's it?"

"That's all I can think of. It was busy today, so I didn't really pay her much attention."

"All right. Casey, you have anything to add?"

"No. I got here shortly before closing and never even saw Miss Tait."

He pointed at Jamie. "What about you, young lady? The JP said Miss Tait talked to you about chest pains?"

Jamie hopped from the car and stood shuffling her feet, her teeth still biting nervously at her nails. "Yes, sir."

Monah reached over and pulled Jamie's hand from her mouth. Much more chewing and she'd be bleeding.

Mike tapped his pencil on the notebook. "Care to expound on that for me?"

Jamie shrugged. "Not much more to say." She sent a guilty glance toward Monah. "My cell phone rang, and I forgot about Miss Tait till Officer Parker asked me a bunch of questions." She paused. "It was my boyfriend who called."

Mike frowned. "Why are you still here, Jamie? Or better, why *were* you still here?"

"I was waiting for my boyfriend. Scared me to death when the ambulance pulled into the parking lot right next to me."

"Who's your boyfriend?"

Fear raced over Jamie's face. "Ah, Corey Adams."

"The young man who assists the janitor at the high school? Isn't he about twenty-three?"

"Um, yeah." Again with the nail chewing. "Can I go now?"

Mike jotted some notes. "Sure. I'll find you if I have more questions." He motioned over his shoulder with his thumb. "I'm going to spend a few more minutes in the ladies' restroom, just to look things over one last time."

"Need any help?" Monah asked hopefully.

Regret coarsened Mike's features. "Sorry, Monah. I can't let you." He leaned closer, and his voice dropped. "You can stick around, though. I won't be long. Wait in my car."

Noise from the edge of the parking lot drew their attention.

"Hey, Mike, would you tell this guy to let me pass?"

Monah grinned at the struggle going on between Officer Parker and Luke Kerrigan. The young lawman sure took his job seriously. He stood with feet braced and his hand on Luke's chest. Taller by a few inches, Luke peered over the man's head at them.

"Let him by, Parker. He's all right." Humor sparkled from Mike's eyes, but his voice was pure authority. "Causing trouble, Luke?"

Luke rushed to Casey's side and wrapped her in his arms.

"Only to Officer Parker, it seems."

Warmth flooded Monah's heart. Luke and Casey were so sweet together, so tender and loving. Luke had probably been worried sick when he heard what had happened. She averted her gaze and slid a few steps closer to Mike.

His fingers grazed her arm. "You all right?"

She forced a smile when he wouldn't look away. "I'll be fine. I just—" Her gaze shifted to the library. "I can still see her lying in there."

He pulled her close, his body warm against the sudden chill that raised goose bumps on her flesh. "I'm sorry, Monah. I wish I'd gotten here sooner." His husky voice made her shiver, and he rubbed her arms. "You sure you're okay? You're a little pale."

She nodded. "I wish you didn't have to work tonight."

"You and me both. Unfortunately, once I wrap it up here, I've still got to go on my stakeout." He tipped her chin up. "Don't change your plans with Casey and Luke. I'd rather you stay with someone for a while."

How did he know she planned to do just that? "All right."

He dropped his hand and pulled a pair of latex gloves from his back pocket. "I'd better get started." He swung around to look at Luke. "You two mind waiting with Monah a minute?"

Luke tugged Monah to his side and dropped his arm across her shoulders. "Not a problem."

"Thanks. I'm gonna take one last look around, and then I'll meet you out here."

"Mike, what about tomorrow?" Monah grabbed his arm. "We'll be able to open, right?"

His hesitation spoke volumes. "Not likely. Bill's going to want to make sure the crime-scene unit's been over everything thoroughly. Once he's satisfied, he'll open up the perimeter, but we might be looking at a day or two."

Disappointment settled onto Monah's chest like an elephant. The last thing a struggling library needed was to close indefinitely, but that was insignificant compared to how Miss Tait's family would feel when they got news of her death. "Does Bill have an idea how Miss Tait died?" She cringed. She sounded just like the crowd from earlier.

Mike shrugged. "At first observation, he thinks it could be a heart attack. It'll take an autopsy to know for sure."

She shuddered again. "When do you think it will be done?"

Mike snorted. "The medical examiner hasn't been too busy lately. I imagine he'll rush over here and have his knife out shortly after Miss Tait is on the table."

Monah grimaced.

"Oh, sorry, Monah. That was stupid. A bit too graphic."

"It's all right." But it wasn't. His words made her tremble.

Mike grabbed her hand and gave it a squeeze. "Wait for me. I'll be back soon."

At her nod, he turned and bolted up the library steps. Monah glanced at her watch. He'd said he wouldn't be long, but with the evening sun casting shadowy fingers across the lawn, he couldn't get back soon enough.

~

Mike emerged from the darkened library almost thirty minutes later, a plastic bag with a half-full water bottle inside in his hand. Monah's heart lifted at the sight of him. The ambulance carrying Miss Tait had long since gone, and except for a few cars, the parking lot was quiet and empty. She pushed off the side of Mike's car, her action alerting Luke and Casey, who had given up trying to talk to her and were whispering quietly to each other.

"There he is," Casey said.

Monah's gaze fixed on the water bottle. "What's that?"

"I found it in the bathroom next to the sink. This the kind you gave her?"

"That's the kind I bought."

He nodded. "Okay. I'm going to give it to the lab techs, just in case."

In case what? She didn't have time to ask. Mike peeled off his gloves and dropped them into a disposal bag hooked to the dashboard of his car.

"Monah, did Miss Tait have a purse? We found her wallet and a tote bag but not her purse."

Her heart thumped. "Um, I don't know." She searched her memory. Nothing. "I'm sorry, Mike. I don't remember."

"That's all right. She may have used something else, like the tote bag." With the water bottle and gloves safely stashed inside the car, he slammed the door shut and adjusted his shirt sleeves. "I think that should do it."

"So? Anything new?" Luke's face reflected her own curiosity.

Mike shrugged. "Nope, but I'd rather Monah didn't drive alone tonight. You guys mind following her home?" Both Luke and Casey gave a quick shake of their heads. Mike put his hand on her lower back as they headed to Monah's car. She loved it when he did that.

Casey pulled a cell phone from her purse. "I should call Aunt Liddy. She'd rather hear about this from me than one of her neighbors."

Mike nodded. "Okay, guys. I've got to head out to another case. Don't let her"—he pointed to Monah—"talk you out of doing something tonight." He turned to her and ran his hand down her arm, ending by squeezing her hand. "I'll call you later." He gave her a final nod and wink before climbing into his car. His departure sucked the last bit of energy from Monah's body. She sagged against the car door, fighting back tears as she watched his taillights disappear around the corner.

"C'mon, Monah. Let's get you home," Casey said.

Whump.

A scream rose in Monah's throat, and she whirled to stare at the library. A small red form, still visible in the fading light, hovered in front of the tall windows. Over and over, it beat against the glass, trying to get inside. Dumb cardinal. It had scared her to death. Luke laughed, and Casey grabbed Monah's hand.

"You know," Luke said, shoving both hands into his pockets, "I could bring one of Mrs. Teaser's cats over here."

Casey swatted him. "Ugh. That's terrible."

He shrugged. "Just trying to help. Monah? What do you say?"

Pity for the bird filled her as she watched it bash into the window. Just because they couldn't understand why it acted as it did didn't mean they should do it harm. Miss Tait's face came to mind, and she shook her head.

"No, just leave it alone. Maybe it'll figure out it's only fighting itself." She hitched her purse strap higher onto her shoulder. "Let's go. Anyone mind if we skip the movie?"

Luke put his arms around both women's shoulders. "Not at all. How about we grab a pizza and go to your house? We can have a nice, quiet night."

"Perfect."

She peeked one last time at the officer on duty at the library entrance then turned her back on the nightmare, hoping she wouldn't have one of her own that night.

CHAPTER ⚏⚏ THREE

"Thanks for coming, Mike."

The door to the examination room of the county morgue closed behind Mike with a sharp click. Fluorescent lights hummed overhead. Sterile air and the stench of formaldehyde pricked his nostrils. Stainless steel drawers lined the wall down one side of the room. He hated this place. It was too. . .lifeless. "No problem. What'd you find?"

Ted Levy, the medical examiner, tugged a spiral notebook and pencil from the pocket of his starched lab coat. "Not a whole lot, actually. I'm preparing a report now, but I wanted to double-check some facts first." He led the way to a steel counter where jars of cotton balls, tweezers, microscope slides, and other items rested beside a manila folder. He slid it toward Mike. "The police report says the deceased was last seen between 3:30 and 4:00?"

"Right, and Monah Trenary found her around 5:15. Why?"

He shrugged. "Go over the witness statements with me again. What were her symptoms?"

Mike ticked them off on his fingers. "Chest pain, nausea, dizziness, sweating, pallor, among other things. Why?"

"Doesn't add up." Ted slid his wire-rimmed glasses up and rubbed the side of his head with his thumb. "Any other visible signs?"

Hip against the counter, Mike crossed his arms and studied the medical examiner. "Where are you going with this?"

Adjusting his glasses, Ted pointed to an item on the page. "You're describing classic symptoms of a heart attack, but what I found contradicts that. This woman was healthy, strong. There's no visible trauma to the heart, and the arteries look good. I found foam in her throat, as though she suffered from respiratory distress. And get this—there's facial paralysis. It just doesn't add up."

Mike picked up Ted's report, scanned the first few lines, and then peered over the page at him. "She was dead for some time before Miss Trenary found her. Could it have been rigor mortis setting in?"

"Rigor was still in the earliest stages."

"What about a stroke?"

Again Ted shook his head. "Brain looks good."

Mike lifted a brow. "So what are you trying to tell me?"

Shoulders bent, Ted leaned against the counter and fingered the spiral wire on his notebook. "She was sick before she died. Bill found vomit on the toilet rim and floor. Now, it's possible that she experienced nausea before having a heart attack. But she ate a pretty large meal for somebody who wasn't feeling well."

"Excuse me?"

"If she ate lunch, got sick, and died all within four or five hours, that means she went downhill pretty fast."

"What about food poisoning?"

"Not likely. Her age puts her at higher risk, but unless she ate contaminated shellfish or mushrooms, there wasn't enough time for that to kill her, because it takes fast food five or six hours to leave the stomach, and the vomitus showed undigested food."

Mike plunked the folder down. "I'm running out of ideas

here, Ted. You're going to have to spell it out."

"Stomach contents looked like hamburger and fries, and while she could get sick from bad beef, death only occurs in a very small percentage of people and usually because of complications from dehydration. The normal two to six hours for symptoms to manifest aren't long enough for dehydration to have occurred." He rubbed his chin with his thumb. "Although, I did have this case once where improper home canning caused a fatal bout of botulism. Who'd have thought canned oysters could smell so bad?"

Mike eyed him with disgust. "Your job is gross."

"Like yours isn't? I'll take dead bodies over drug dealers and crime lords any day."

A low chuckle rumbled in Mike's chest. "Okay. What else?"

Ted pulled open the drawer where Miss Tait's covered form lay. "A wound to the cranium. The lack of significant bleeding tells me something besides head trauma killed her."

"So, she was already in trouble when she fell."

"Right."

"And that brings us right back to natural causes." Parker wouldn't be happy.

Using the tip of his pencil, Ted scratched his wrinkled brow. "It's looking like it. Still, I'd like to order a toxicology report." He shrugged. "It's just a hunch, but I'd like to follow it up."

Unease stirred in Mike's gut. "Are you telling me you think she was poisoned?"

Ted's gaze remained steady. "Like I said, it's just a hunch."

Mike had learned long ago to trust Ted's hunches. At sixty-one, the wily medical examiner had seen and learned more in his lifetime than Mike wanted to know. Maybe it was just Ted's inquisitive nature that prompted him to dig deeper for a cause of death, and maybe it wasn't. Mike wasn't taking any chances. "Do it. I'll let Bill know what's going on."

Ted nodded and scooped up the pages scattered over the counter. "Results could be two or three weeks getting back. I'll call you when they come in."

"Thanks, Ted."

Mike pushed out of the examination room, the responsibilities of his job weighing heavily on his chest. Bad enough the police department had an arsonist running around town setting fires in abandoned buildings. Now they might find themselves dealing with a murderer? He looked heavenward. How much more could their small town take?

~

Monah pulled into the library parking lot early the next morning, glad to see Mike's car still there. She had stopped by the police station. The officer manning the counter told her where to find him. The crime tape draped around the library flapped in the breeze, almost as if waving her off from approaching. She ignored the thought. She was on a mission.

She hoped Mike was there to tear down the tape so she could reopen. If not, maybe he'd let her get her laptop so she could get some work done at home. It was worth a try.

Mike swung through the door just as she reached the steps. He smiled and motioned for her to wait. After turning to lock up, he stuck a paper across both glass doors, the heading warning all interested parties that it was illegal to break the seal. Her heart dropped.

"I guess we don't get to open today, huh?"

He pocketed the key and descended the steps. "Sorry, Monah. Not today."

"Tomorrow?"

One corner of his mouth pulled into a frown. "Doubtful. In fact, don't count on opening till the day after tomorrow. That will give us plenty of time to tie up any loose ends."

"Two days?" She stared with longing at her home away from home. "You sure you can't get everything done today?"

Feeling a light tug on her hair, she turned to find Mike smiling at her, some of her hair still clasped between his fingers. He let it slip free. "Why the hurry? I thought you'd enjoy a couple of days off. You looked a little stressed yesterday."

"Well, I'm not looking forward to all the lookey-loos, but I'd hate to see the library shut down for too long."

"Because. . . ?"

"Monah?" Dena Drolen, dressed in a stylish pantsuit with purse and heels to match, headed their way.

"Oh great."

Mike followed her gaze. "What?"

"Dena. She'll be wanting her mail."

"Huh?"

"That rotten postal worker. Either he enjoys seeing Dena in a dither, or he's too lazy to do his job correctly."

Dena drew up beside them and pulled Monah into a tight hug. "Are you all right? Is there anything I can do? I couldn't believe it when I heard the news."

"No, I think everything is under control."

Dena was a small woman, even in two-inch heels. Her silky hair tickled Monah's chin, and the scent of fine perfume drifted to her nose. Over her shoulder, Monah saw a car moving slowly by. Sandy? Sure enough. With the window rolled down, her co-worker's curious face was visible. Monah waved her in. Sandy pulled into a parking spot several yards away.

"I'm sorry, Dena," Monah said, stepping out of the hug. "I

appreciate you thinking of me today, but I can't stay. Do you mind?"

"Not at all," she said with a wave of her hand. "Go on. I'll catch up with you later." She turned her attention to Mike, and Monah had no doubt she'd keep him wrapped up asking questions for several minutes.

Seizing the opportunity, Monah trotted over to meet Sandy. "I guess you heard about Miss Tait?"

Sandy peered past her and nodded. "I tried to call, but you didn't answer."

Monah patted her pocket. Empty. "I must have forgotten my cell phone in the car." She glanced at Mike and then turned back. "You want to stay for a while? I know this is disturbing."

"No. I mean, I just wondered if I needed to come in to work."

Seemed to be the question of the day. "Not until Friday. That's what Mike just told me."

"Hi, Sandy."

Monah stood upright at the sound of Mike's voice. He sure was light on his feet for such a tall man. He leaned down to look in the window. Over his shoulder, Monah saw Dena tapping her foot with impatience.

"You doing all right?"

Sandy nodded, her lips a curious shade of pale.

"Have you got a moment? I need to question you about yesterday."

"Why?"

"I'll be talking to everyone who was at the library. Do you mind?"

"Not at all. Just let me know when."

Her knuckles were white from gripping the steering wheel so tightly. Mike must be making her nervous. He even made *her* nervous when he looked like that, and they were dating.

He tapped the car door. "Why don't you head to the police station now? I'll be right behind you."

He stood and briefly grasped Monah's arm. "I'll call you later. If I find you can open earlier than Friday, I'll let you know."

"Thanks."

He patted the roof of Sandy's car then veered toward his own.

Traffic had picked up. Several cars, only feet apart, drove past. Some pulled into the parking lot for a closer look. One of the drivers even took pictures. Monah rolled her eyes. This was only the beginning. Things were going to be miserable when she finally could open. The laptop! She'd forgotten the reason she'd tracked Mike down.

"Stay here a minute, Sandy." She raced across the short distance to his car. "Wait, Mike. Is it possible to let me in so I can get my laptop?"

Dena had finally given up waiting for Mike and moved to leave, but at Monah's question, she paused with one leg half in and half out of her silver Mercedes. "If you're going inside, can I get my mail?"

Mike shook his head. "Sorry, ladies. The library stays locked up with everything intact until we're sure we've checked it all out."

Dena made a face but then smiled. "That's all right. I don't like getting bills anyway." She gave them a wave. "I'll see you later, Monah. Let me know if you need my help with anything."

Monah barely gave notice to Dena's farewell. She peered at Mike. "Does that mean you can't go into my office and get my laptop for me?"

"That's what it means." He reached out and squeezed her hand. "Why don't you just use this free time to go home and do some reading?"

She propped her hands on her hips. "Because all the books are in the *library*."

His lips twitched. She narrowed her eyes at him. "Don't you dare laugh."

Hands up in surrender, he had the gall to smile. "I'm sorry, Monah." He inclined his head toward Sandy. "I've got to go." He paused with his fingers curled around the door handle of his car. "By the way, you look really nice."

He didn't wait for a response but winked and climbed inside. Of all the nerve. Toss a compliment her way and then disappear. She could have used a hug.

"Monah?"

Oh yeah. Sandy. "Sorry." She returned to the car. "I just wanted to make sure you were all right. You seemed a little uptight."

"I know. I just. . ." She glanced up at the library and then put her hand on her cheek. "Oh, Monah, poor Charlotte. I know we didn't exactly get along, but I still feel bad. What an awful thing."

"Yes, it is."

A quick honk grabbed their attention. Mike was pulling onto the street. She waved at him.

"You'd better go. I'll talk to you later."

Monah stood in the parking lot for several minutes. Except for the cars driving by, she was alone. She'd never felt so muddled, so disjointed. The library couldn't open soon enough.

CHAPTER FOUR

The library couldn't close soon enough.

Monah sat at the counter shuffling library cards and trying to look busy. If only she could find her pencil. It was on the desk a minute ago. Rummaging through the clutter, she patted a stack of papers. The clicking of the ceiling fan overhead didn't usually bother her, but today the noise mingled with a steady flow of whispers and drove her to distraction.

Just as she'd expected the first day back after Miss Tait's death, the library filled up the moment she opened the doors. Some of the bolder visitors raced toward the ladies' room. Others bombarded her with questions. She stopped their queries by telling them she knew nothing more than what they'd seen in the newspaper. Somehow, one of them snatched her copy from the counter-top without her noticing. Irritated, she tossed the remainder of her mocha cappuccino in the trash can. Caffeine could be danger-ous to her patrons' health today. Thank goodness it was Friday so she could close early.

To make matters worse, Mike had called and said he'd be there soon—they needed to talk. Under normal circumstances, the news would have excited her. Today, a nervous knot settled in her stomach and tightened with each passing minute. Where was Casey? She'd promised to swing by and help calm her frazzled nerves.

"Monah?"

She jumped, upsetting the pencil cup poised on the edge of her desk. The contents spilled to the floor with a clatter. Dena Drolen stood at the counter, her elbows and shoulder bag planted on top.

"I'm so sorry. I didn't mean to startle you." Dena's brow furrowed, and a sad frown pulled at her perfectly lined lips. "I can come back."

Monah shook her head and bent to pick up the pencils. "No need. You checking on your mail?"

"Yes, and to see if you're all right." She glanced around. "I figured this would happen. I bet not one of this bunch has even signed out a book."

Monah grimaced. "No. I guess this was the best place to congregate and gather information to spread around town." She bit her tongue. No good could come of spewing her annoyance and impatience. "Let me look in the office to see if anything came for you."

"Thank you."

At her desk, Monah quickly sorted out the month's bills and set them aside. The junk mail she dumped in the trash can. Not even a postcard. She headed back out.

"Sorry, Dena. Looks like you made the trip for nothing."

"Oh, that's all right. I'm on my way to the grocery store, so it was no bother. Thanks for checking. Maybe one day we'll get the postman straightened out. Anyway, hope the day gets better for you." With a quick wave, she glided toward the door, holding it for Sandy, who was just on her way in.

"I'm so sorry I'm late, Monah. I stopped by the bakery for doughnuts"—she lifted the box—"and got caught up in all the chatter about Miss Tait. I didn't know you were the one to find her. How awful." She set the box down and drew her into a hug. "Anything I can do?"

All eyes centered on them. Monah pulled away and motioned to the office with her head. They moved inside and shut the door.

"You're going to have to refrain from talking about it while you're here, Sandy. I don't want this place to become gossip central."

Sandy opened the bottom drawer of the desk and dropped her purse inside. "Oh, of course. I wouldn't want that either. My lips are sealed." She locked her lips and dropped the invisible key down the front of her flowered blouse. She shoved the drawer closed with her foot and plopped into the chair. "But just for my own sake, dear, would you tell me what happened? How you found her? You know, all that stuff."

A soft tap kept her from having to answer—another blessing. Mike smiled at her through the glass in the door, and her heart skipped a beat. How did he manage to look so good when things were so bad?

He cracked the door open. "Now a good time?"

"Of course." She turned to Sandy. "Would you excuse us?"

"Sure thing, dear. Don't you worry." Sandy hoisted to her feet. "I'll take care of things while you're busy." She brushed past Mike as she left the room and must have taken all the air with her, for Monah found it tough to breathe. Her chest tight and palms sweaty, she stared at Mike's chest.

He tipped her chin up until their eyes met. "Did you get any sleep last night?"

She swallowed hard and tried to smile. "A little. Not much. Enough, I guess."

One corner of his mouth tilted up. "Well, which is it?"

She shrugged. "I got all I could."

"I was afraid of that." He wrapped his arms around her for a brief hug. "I'm sorry, Monah. I'll try to make this as easy as possible." After she nodded, he stepped to the window beside her desk and opened the blinds, surprising her. From this vantage, she overlooked row upon row of towering library shelves. Patrons could clearly see her as well. Mike shrugged. "I don't want anyone to get the wrong idea. You've got enough to deal with."

If she'd had any doubts about the kind of man Mike was, he just put them to rest. Some of the tension lifted from her shoulders, and for the first time that morning, she didn't have to force a smile. "Thank you."

He motioned to the two leather club chairs she had picked up at a yard sale, and they took a seat. Reaching inside his jacket, he withdrew a small spiral notebook and flipped it open.

"I've got some news for you, something I'd like you to keep to yourself. Then I have more questions."

"Okay." The arms of her chair were smooth and hard beneath her curled fingers. She hated when he switched into cop mode. He was harder to read, less like the Mike she knew and trusted.

His perfectly creased navy khakis rustled as he crossed his long legs. "I talked to Ted Levy. He said Miss Tait's heart showed no signs of illness or abnormality."

Shock, surprise, curiosity—all three rolled through her. "Well, what did she die from then?"

"He's not sure. He's ordered more tests."

Mike didn't offer any details, nor did it look as if he planned to. Lacing her fingers to keep from fidgeting, Monah resisted the urge to probe. "You said you had questions?"

"Yes." He checked his notebook. "Did Miss Tait have anything to eat or drink while she was here, besides the water you gave her?"

She strained to remember, her heart thumping hard again. "I don't think so, unless she brought something with her. You've got to understand, Mike—I don't keep that close an eye on everyone when it's busy. You saw what it was like when you came in." She crossed and uncrossed her legs, sat up in the chair, then slouched back down. "People bring in bags and purses and—"

"Monah."

Her fingers plucked nervously at her hair. "—there's no telling what all—"

He grabbed her fingers and squeezed. "Monah. Take a breath."

She stopped and did as she was told, dropping her hand in her lap when she saw his smile.

"It was just a question. I've got to cover everything."

Heat radiated from her face. She blathered on like that far too often. "Sure. I'm sorry."

"No problem." He leaned back in his seat. "Okay, before we go any further, did you happen to come up with anything— anything at all—that you forgot to tell me about that day?"

"No, I think I told you all of it."

"Good." He flipped to another page of his notebook. "Now, I know Officer Parker took down a list of names of everyone who was here at the same time as Miss Tait, but I'd like to go over it again, just to make sure we didn't miss anyone."

A list of patrons. Her mouth went dry. "Mike, do you suspect foul play?"

Shuttered. That was the only way to explain the look in his eyes.

"I just don't want to miss any steps in the process."

Her skin prickled with apprehension, but he looked calm and completely relaxed. She tried in vain to take her cue from him. The case of water under the desk caught her eye, and she reached for a bottle. After several swallows, she felt better.

"Sorry." She wiped a drop from her bottom lip with the tip of her finger.

"Take your time."

"Okay, let's see. Sandy and I were working, of course. And you know Jamie was also here."

"And Casey."

She stared at him, more than a little confused. "Not until shortly before closing. She told you that."

"Right. Who else?"

Tension crept its way up her spine as she played through the afternoon in her mind. "Well, Jimmy Capps worked on the air conditioner. Ken came in to do an inspection. Um, oh yeah— Mr. Dyer stopped in to pick up his son." The vision of him and Miss Tait exchanging words played through her memory. Should she say something to him? "Ah, he and Miss Tait spent a little time talking."

Mike's brows bunched into a troubled frown. "At her table?"

"Yes."

"Did you hear any of their conversation?"

"No, but neither one looked happy, especially when he pulled out his wallet."

"Really?" Mike's pencil scratched across the pages of his notebook. "All right, who else?"

"All Miss Tait's students."

"Name them off for me if you can."

She blew out a long, unsteady breath. "Paul Dyer, Ashley Knight, Jason Sasser, Tyler Jeffries, Linda Minton, Beth what's-her-name, um, Wescott." She ticked them off on her fingers so as not to forget any of them. "Jill Spencer and Matt Collier." She met Mike's gaze. "Seems like there's one more." She closed her eyes and replayed them walking in. "Oh, and Debbie Litton."

He finished writing the names. "Anyone else you can think of?"

"Robin Beck and her daughter, Lauren, spent most of the afternoon here." She pushed her glasses up on her nose. "And you."

His head jerked up, and a slow smile curved his lips. "Yeah. Wish I could have stayed longer."

"Me, too."

He turned to the next page in his notebook. "One last thing, probably the hardest part of this."

Uncrossing his legs, he leaned forward and rested his elbows on his knees. He no longer looked comfortable, which made her distinctly uncomfortable. She needed something to do with her hands. She grabbed a lock of her hair and twisted it around her finger.

"Did you and Miss Tait exchange words?"

No response would come, could come with her tongue stuck to the roof of her mouth. She took another drink of water and had to force her throat to swallow. *He thinks I'm a suspect.*

"Words?" She croaked it out like a smoker with a bad cold.

He tucked the notebook into his pocket. "Everyone knows about the, shall we say, animosity between you two. You've both been vocal about the funds donated to the city last month. I thought I'd better ask and get it out in the open before the media and gossips set it aflame. If I know everything beforehand, I'll be better able to keep the rumors from getting out of control." He opened his hands in a helpless gesture before folding them in front of him. "So, did you two argue?"

Nervousness fluttered inside Monah's belly. She reached up, patted her head, and pulled two pencils from her hair. Blood rushed to her face. She refused to look at him.

"Do you plan to answer my question? Did you two argue?"

"Sort of."

"What does that mean?"

One pencil slid from her fingers and dropped onto the floor. She sat back and crossed her arms. "Miss Tait attacked me for how cold I had it in here. Said she'd be sure to let the city council know of my disregard for proper spending of city money so they wouldn't give me any more. I tried to explain about the air conditioner being broken, but I don't think she believed me. She said I'd be held responsible for—" She gasped and clenched the arms of her chair at what she'd been about to say.

"Responsible for what?"

Her hand shook as she put her fingers to her mouth.

"Monah?"

The tightness in her chest radiated through every muscle in her body. "For catching her death. That's what she said."

He leaned toward her. "Monah—"

A bright light flashed from the window in the door. A photographer peered through the blinds and snapped another picture. Monah rose from her chair. Why didn't Sandy stop him? Mike rushed out of the office. Monah joined him just as he jerked the camera from the man's hands.

"What do you think you're doing, Schultz?" Mike growled.

Louis Schultz. Monah despised his type of paparazzi reporting. He made a grab for his camera. Mike pulled it away and hit the DELETE button before Schultz could protest.

Schultz planted his chubby fists on his hips. "She's a suspect, isn't she? I have every right to take any picture I want."

Mike frowned. "We have not named any suspects. Nothing has been determined in Miss Tait's death. You have no reason to think there's a story here."

"That's not what I heard."

The library door slammed open, and Casey rushed toward them, her cheeks flushed from running. "Mike! The warehouse is on fire."

"What warehouse?"

"Bill. . .Bing. . ." Casey's hands fluttered through the air. "I don't know."

"Bingham's?"

"That's it."

Mike shoved the camera into the photographer's chest and ran out of the library without a backward glance.

CHAPTER FIVE

Monah grabbed Casey's arm, stopping her from heading toward the door along with half the library crowd. "Where are you going?"

Casey swung around, her expression telling Monah the answer should be evident. "To the fire."

"You can't. I need you."

Understanding dawned on Casey's face. She glanced at the door then turned back with eyes wide. "What'd Mike say?"

With her finger to her lips, Monah looked around to make sure no one heard. Too late. The few people who remained were watching them curiously. A couple at the door even turned back inside. She motioned Casey toward the office and followed, pausing at Sandy's side.

"Do you mind taking the counter again? I want to talk to Casey, and there are way too many ears out there, all aimed in my direction." She said it loud enough for everyone to hear, but rather than take the hint and move away, they only smiled.

Sandy stood. "Okay, but I wouldn't mind hearing some of what the detective said. You know, inquiring minds and all." She tapped her temple, then broke off with an embarrassed grin and closed the door.

Mike's questions raced through Monah's mind. "You're not

going to believe this." She sat in the chair next to Casey, then jumped up when she couldn't be still. She paced to the far wall and back again. "Mike thinks—"

A good many of the patrons had their noses pressed against the window behind the counter, Sandy included. Giving each of them a scowl, Monah spun the rod to close the blinds.

"You'd think they'd at least try to be a little less obvious."

Casey grasped her shirttail and tugged her down into the nearest seat. "Never mind them. Tell me everything Mike said."

Trying not to smile, Monah raised a brow and crossed her arms. "You're leaving a nose print on my window, Case."

"What?"

Monah gestured outside where the curious patrons were milling around her office. With a grin, Casey swatted at her. "Quit stalling and spill it."

"Okay." Monah grasped the arm of the chair and leaned close. "Mike suspects foul play."

Casey's mouth formed a shocked little O. "So this isn't just a simple case of a heart attack or something similar? Are they talking murder?"

"They're still not sure. He said Ted Levy is ordering more tests." She thumped the armrest. "Can you believe he has me on his list of 'people of interest'? He questioned *me*."

"Of course he questioned you, silly. He'll probably question me and half the other residents in this town who were at the library that day. That's all part of Mike's job. Tell me what else he said."

And here she thought Casey would be as appalled as she felt. She slumped in the chair. "He asked if I had words with Miss Tait."

"You told him you did?"

She let out a long sigh and pushed up from the chair. "Of course. I couldn't lie." Lifting her thumbnail to her teeth, she resumed pacing. She stopped when Casey pulled her Post-its from her purse, a sure sign she planned on getting involved. "I was hoping you'd help."

Casey grinned up at her. "You know I love a good mystery." She patted the chair beside her, and Monah dropped back onto it. "All right, give me the same list of suspects Mike has."

As Monah recited them, Casey wrote them on her pad, tearing off two and sticking them to her chair before listing the last one. Her brow furrowed as she concentrated, then cleared as she leaned forward and scratched through several names.

"What are you doing?"

"Crossing out the people we know aren't guilty so we can focus on the others." Casey tapped the eraser against her chin. "Let's see. We know it's not you, me, or Sandy, and probably not Jamie since she wasn't here much." The tip of her pencil hovered over Jimmy Capps's name. "What about him?"

"No way. He spent all his time working on the air-conditioning unit. He had no contact whatsoever with Miss Tait."

Casey gave her an *Are you sure?* look.

"I'm sure."

With a scrape of pencil lead, the list shortened by one more. "Any others I should cross off, or should we get to work on the rest of these?"

Casting suspicion on anyone didn't set well. How many times did she cringe at the idea that others thought poorly of her? Wouldn't she be doing the very same thing? Still, it surely couldn't hurt to help the police with their investigation. Who better than the two women who had experience solving crimes?

Feeling a little better about pointing fingers, she nodded.

"We'll need to check on the rest of the list, though I doubt we need to spend much time on the students. I think every kid who ever graduated from that school hoped Miss Tait would quit teaching, but I can't imagine any of us wished her dead."

"She was really that bad?"

Monah smiled. "Probably not. I learned a lot from her, and I'm thankful for that. She just seemed so mean and grouchy all the time. Very strict. She got a lot of students in trouble by sending them to the principal's office. You know how kids react to that."

Casey raised her brows. "Yeah. They hope the teacher disappears and never comes back."

~

Flames licked at the warehouse windows. Mike reached for the car door handle, a sick feeling in his gut. If he'd been here, instead of wrapped up at the library. . .

Stumbling on rutted breaks where clumps of grass poked through the pavement, volunteer firemen scrambled across the lot. Mike circled around them to look for Ken. Radio in hand, the fire chief peered up through thick coils of black smoke.

"Tell the men to concentrate most of the water on the back side," Ken barked into the handset. "Keep the worst of it away from the other buildings." He glanced over as Mike walked up. "Hey, Mike."

"Can I help?"

"Not likely. Maybe if we had a real fire department with up-to-date equipment, we could have responded in time." He shook his head. "Most we can hope for is to keep it from spreading. The warehouse itself is a loss."

Mike turned with him to watch the old building choke out its final breaths in gray, roiling clouds. "Were there any witnesses?"

"None."

"Who called it in?"

"Lady who lives down the road. Said she saw an orange glow. By the time we got here, the place was engulfed."

With the exception of Ken and him, the mood was unexpectedly light. *Joke in the face of danger*, Mike thought with a grunt. Once the fire at the rear of the building was sufficiently contained, the firemen hooted and shouted, barks of laughter mingling with the crackling and popping of burning wood and heated steel. Somebody would undoubtedly be buying a round of drinks tonight.

Mike shoved his hands into his pockets. "What do you think?"

"It was an eyesore. The town will probably be better off without the rattrap."

Neither man looked at the other. Sparks fluttered into the sky like a thousand angry fireflies. Mike waited and watched. "Is that all?"

"We'll have to wait until it cools down enough to be sure."

"But you're suspicious?"

Ken shrugged. "An abandoned warehouse on the edge of town? Yeah, I'm suspicious. It's not like we've had an unusually dry summer or lightning that could have sparked something off."

"Vandals, maybe? Teenagers with too much time on their hands?"

Ken pushed his fireman's hat back on his head and focused his steady gaze on him. "If it weren't for the other fires. . ."

"I know." Mike clenched his jaw. Ken didn't have to say it. If it weren't for the other fires, they might chalk this one up as an accident. Instead, it was one more on a mounting list. "So why is the person doing it, and how do we catch him?"

"He'll mess up eventually." Ken cast a quick glance around. Mike did likewise. Now that the fire was under control, no one seemed to be paying much attention. "We'll just have to keep our eyes and ears open, see what turns up."

"Anything in particular we need to be looking for?" He followed Ken through the maze of vehicles and equipment to Ken's car.

Stripping off his flame-retardant coat, Ken threw it, along with his hat, onto the backseat. "It would help if we knew what the arsonist was using as an accelerant. That way, we'd be able to figure out where he's getting his supplies. Unfortunately, the set-up has varied every time. Makes me think it could be more than one person."

"Or maybe it's one very smart arsonist who's doing everything he can to keep from getting caught. Somebody who knows exactly what the fire department would be looking for."

Slamming the door shut, Ken paused with his hand on the roof, his eyes speculative. "You're not saying it's one of my guys?"

"Nope, just somebody who hangs around with one of your guys, or somebody with a grudge against one of them. It's a possibility."

He gave a slow nod. "Okay, I can buy that. Let me think on it. I'll see what I come up with and have the information to you by tomorrow morning."

A cloud of frustration settling heavily on his chest, Mike shook Ken's hand and then walked to his car. There was nothing more he could do here. He'd better get back to the station so he could start filing his report with the state fire marshal.

CHAPTER SIX

Monah jumped out of her chair and grabbed the water bottle from her desk. Casey's comment about students hoping their teacher disappeared and never came back hit her right in the throat. She took a sip to wash the feeling away, but the lump remained.

How many times had she wished some of her teachers would disappear, along with a lot of the students? Being new to a school wasn't easy, and Monah had a tendency to talk too much when she got nervous, a fact that often inspired ridicule. When she started wearing glasses soon after her arrival, the teasing became almost unbearable. The teachers rarely bothered to silence the criticism. They always had their favorites. It wasn't until popular Luke Kerrigan befriended her that things changed, though the feelings of inferiority still surfaced from time to time. But never once in all those years could she remember wanting to do any of her teachers harm. Well, other than a punch in the nose once in a while.

"You okay?" Casey's eyes flashed with concern.

Monah snapped out of her reminiscing and focused on the suspect list.

"I can't seem to wrap my mind around the possibility of one of the kids killing someone." She leaned against the edge of the desk and set her water down. "Just how likely is it that a teen actually murdered Miss Tait?"

Casey shrugged. "I don't know. Years ago I would have answered 'not at all,' but look at the school violence lately, bomb threats and shootings, mostly by teens. It sure makes you think, doesn't it?"

"Oh man. I never thought about it like that." She rubbed beneath the nosepieces of her glasses and then pushed them back in place. The whole conversation was a bit overwhelming. "All right, so if we were to pick the most likely kid to do someone harm, who would it be?"

"I don't think we can look at it that way. Desperate situations can force desperate acts." Casey tapped the list of names. "Who had the most to gain by getting rid of Miss Tait?"

Someone knocked at the door. Monah sighed and rose to answer. She expected Sandy, demanding to know what Mike had to say. She didn't expect Paul Dyer.

"Paul."

He gave her his typical condescending smile. "I need to ask you something."

"Sure." She motioned him to enter. "Casey, this is Paul Dyer." She turned her back and raised her brows at Casey who grabbed up the Post-its stuck to the arm of her chair. Relief washed through Monah. Paul was the type who didn't miss much, but Casey managed to hide their notes before he saw them. "He's one of the students at the high school."

"Hi, Paul." Casey picked up her purse. "I should leave you two alone."

No! "Stay put, Case. I doubt this will take long." She looked at Paul. "Right?"

When he nodded, Casey settled in again.

Striving to appear calmer than she felt, Monah leaned against the desk and crossed her arms. "What can I do for you?"

"Do you have the essays we wrote for Miss Tait the other day?"

Why in the world would he want to know that? "No. I think the detective took everything that belonged to her." She had to ask. "Why?"

He shrugged. "My dad told me to make sure they'd be counted for a grade." He leaned past Monah and motioned with his head. "He doesn't want me to have to do the work again." One corner of his mouth turned up in a smirk. "And I don't either."

Through the window, Monah saw Mr. Dyer standing near the front doors. "Why didn't your dad come in?"

Paul grinned and shoved his hands into his pockets. "I think he's kinda freaked out about a dead body being in here. I wouldn't be surprised if he never entered the library again. Not sure I want to come back either."

They acted as if the body were still here. She peered out the window again and caught Mr. Dyer staring. He gave a slight nod before looking away. Monah shared a glance with Casey then faced Paul.

"Like I said, the detective took everything. You'll have to talk to him about it."

"All right. I'll tell Dad that."

Paul sauntered out of the office and through the front doors. He and his father strode to the parking lot with their heads together.

"That was weird." Casey pulled out her Post-its and drew a star next to Paul's and Mr. Dyer's names. "I'm putting them at the top of the list for now." Casey stuck the notes back on the armrest of her chair and poised her pen over the pad. "What do you know about those two? Anything?"

"Well"—Monah grabbed a tissue from the box on the desk, pulled off her glasses, and huffed on the lenses before wiping them—"Mr. Dyer is on the school board."

"How well did he and Miss Tait get along?"

The vision of Mr. Dyer talking to Miss Tait on Wednesday replayed in her mind. He never once seemed happy with the teacher. "Not great." She slid her glasses back in place. "I'm not sure why, other than Miss Tait wasn't easily swayed when it came to grades. She couldn't be bought if the kids weren't doing well."

Casey peered at her, a slight frown puckering her brows. "How do you know all this?"

The question hit Monah right in the stomach. "Um." She didn't want to answer because of how it would make her look. "Most of it I hear from Sandy." The sun could have been right overhead for the burning sensation on her face. *Note to self: Put a stop to the office gossip.* "Some I overhear." Which wasn't any better than gossiping.

Casey only gave a slight nod and looked away. She was a good friend.

"Did you hear anything else we can use?"

Monah scowled at the tiny smile forming on her friend's lips.

Casey shrugged. "Hey, what's done is done. Today's a new day. In the meantime, why not use the information you have if it will help Miss Tait and her family?"

Let off the hook with a sweet reprimand, Monah's defenses melted. "Okay. I need to think a minute."

She meandered around the office trying to recall what she'd heard about the Dyers. Nothing. She stopped at the window and stared outside. What else had Sandy told her?

A car moved slowly through the parking lot. Probably another curious snoop. She paused midturn when the driver circled around. Tyler Jeffries. He was one of the teens in the library with Miss Tait. It didn't appear that he planned to park and come in, but he seemed to be looking for someone. In the next moment, a memory slammed to the fore, and she spun around.

Casey's eyes brightened. "What?"

"I just remembered something." She moved to the other side of the desk. "I overheard part of a conversation between two of the teens while returning books to the shelves."

"Wednesday?"

Monah waved the question away, not wanting her thoughts interrupted. "No. This was earlier in the year."

"What'd they say?"

She gave Casey a big-eyed glare.

Casey raised her hands. "Sorry."

What was it they said? She leaned on the edge of the desk and stared at the floor trying to organize her thoughts. Grades. That was it.

"Tyler was telling Paul about the poor grades he'd received in Miss Tait's class. He said something about not getting a scholarship if he didn't ace the rest of his tests." She looked up at Casey. "He asked Paul if there was anything his dad could do to sway Miss Tait."

"Did he?"

"I don't know." She started pacing in front of the desk again. "You know, there might be a way to find out."

"How?"

"We could check the minutes of the school board meetings. They'd—"

She caught a glimpse of Mike just as he rounded the corner to enter the office. She lunged for the Post-it notes stuck to Casey's chair.

"What are you doing?" The question hadn't fully left Casey's mouth before Mike rapped on the door and entered. Monah put her hands behind her back just as Casey shoved her Post-it pad into her purse.

Mike glanced from one to the other as he shut the door. Monah knew the moment understanding dawned, because Mike closed his eyes, leaned back, and thumped his head against the wall twice. The poor man looked tired.

"Don't even tell me you're getting involved in my case." His eyes bored right into hers.

Monah raised her brows innocently. "What makes you think that?"

Without a word, Mike pushed away from the wall and approached her, a tender smile on his face. As if in slow motion, he reached up and cupped her cheeks in his hands. Oh man. Was he going to kiss her? Right here? In front of Casey? Not that she minded. She'd take one from him any day.

She tilted her head to accept his kiss. In the next instant, he lifted the glasses from her face and took a step back.

"Hey!" She squinted at his blurred face. He knew she couldn't see much without them. "What'd you do that for?"

He dangled the spectacles in front of her. She grabbed for them. He slipped the Post-its from her fingers. "Now you can have your glasses back."

Casey burst into laughter. "He's good."

Monah threw a silencing glare at her friend as she put her glasses on. It worked to keep her from saying more, but the grin remained. She turned her glower on Mike. He paid her no mind as he examined the notes.

"You've got two names starred. Why?"

Ha! Did he really think she would explain after what he just did? She crossed her arms and rested her hip against the desk.

He sidled next to her and bumped her with his elbow. "Hey."

She refused to look at him.

He leaned closer, his face mere inches from hers. "Forgive me?"

His close proximity sent her nerve endings into turmoil, but no way would she let him know that. She cast him a pout. "I'm thinking on it. First I have to get over being mad at myself for letting you trick me." How embarrassing. She reached for the notes. He jerked them away. "Do I get those back?"

"Are these the exact same names you gave me?"

"Yes."

He held them out but wouldn't release them. "Are you going to tell me why those names are starred?"

She finally looked up at him. He had the nicest eyes. No man should be that good looking. "I guess."

He smiled and let them go. Monah and Casey took turns filling him in on what they'd learned. "Casey and I were just talking about checking the minutes of all the school board meetings this year when you walked in, just to see if there was anything unusual." Monah shrugged. "That's about it."

"Good idea. I'll head over there now and see if anyone's in the office."

Monah stood when he did. He stopped. "Whoa. Where do you think you're going?"

"To the school."

He opened his mouth, then clamped it shut again as he examined her face. "I'm not going to be able to talk you out of this, am I? You'll just go on your own, won't you?"

With a tilt of her head, Monah attempted her most innocent expression. Mike groaned and rolled his eyes.

"All right. You can come. But I do all the talking."

Monah glanced back at a smiling Casey and bobbed her eyebrows. "Of course."

"I saw that."

Monah peered up at him. "Saw what?"

He groaned again. "Lord, help me."

CHAPTER SEVEN

Tantalizing as it was, Mike resisted the urge to catch Monah in his arms when she sauntered past, her chin tipped at a jaunty angle. Exactly how was he going to question school personnel when he had such a cute little distraction tagging along?

He pushed open the door and heaved another sigh. "Okay, c'mon. Might as well get this over with."

"While you're at it"—Casey jumped up from her chair—"you may want to ask what the school plans to do about Miss Tait's classes now that she's. . .well. . .deceased."

The door creaked open. "I can answer that."

Mike's head turned along with Monah's and Casey's toward the cheerful voice. Lauren Beck? She smiled brightly at them and hefted the backpack from her shoulder so that it collapsed to the floor with a thump. "Principal Matthews called this morning and asked me to fill in. I'm here collecting the books I'll need to finish the summer English course."

Another bright smile. A tiny seed of suspicion rooted in Mike's brain. If he remembered right, Lauren was fresh out of college and armed with a teaching degree, but her chances of hiring on at the high school were slim to none until Miss Tait retired—or expired, as it happened.

"Congratulations, Lauren," Monah said softly.

Mike knew that tone. He shot her a glance. Her face remained impassive. Not a good sign.

"Yeah, congratulations."

Not Casey, too! Sure enough, a look flew between her and Monah that could only mean trouble. Casey slipped her hand inside her purse and pulled out a yellow Post-it.

Mike snagged Monah's arm and dragged her to the door before Lauren could blink. "Good to see you, Lauren. Wish we could talk. See you around." Outside the office, he whirled to Monah. "What was that all about?"

Huffing to catch her breath, Monah grasped his hands, her eyes flashing with excitement. "Mike, don't you get it? Lauren actually seemed happy that Miss Tait died, and why wouldn't she? She had a lot to gain." Her voice crept up an octave.

Mike cast a quick glance around the crowded library. Several patrons peered over books and magazines at them. "Uh, yeah, can we talk about this in the car?"

"*Oooh.* Right." She winked conspiratorially at him. "Let me tell Sandy I need her to close up." Monah bustled off but returned right away with her purse slung over her shoulder. "All set."

From the corner of his eye, Mike watched her fidget as they walked across the parking lot. What exactly did she think he meant when he said he wanted to wait until they got into the car? It didn't take long to find out. She fairly exploded the moment they climbed inside.

"I'm right, aren't I? Lauren Beck had a lot to gain by Miss Tait's death. We can't rule out her mother, though. Robin was just as upset over her daughter not getting hired as Lauren. Wasn't Lauren a cheerleader in high school? Yeah, I think she was captain or something. You know what they say: Once a cheerleader mom, always a cheerleader mom."

Mike started the engine and gestured silently to Monah's seat belt. She clicked it into place but kept right on talking.

"Did you see that special on TV last week about the Texas woman who tried to kill a student because she thought her daughter wouldn't make the squad otherwise? Crazy, I tell ya, but this falls into exactly the same category."

"Monah?"

"After we finish at the high school, I say we take a spin around the Beck place just to see what Robin has been up to."

Mike leaned toward her, his left arm resting on the steering wheel, the other on the back of the seat behind her head. "Monah."

She froze, and her glasses slipped a fraction of an inch down her nose. "Huh?"

"Are you finished?"

She closed her mouth and nodded.

"Good." He started to pull his arm away, but suddenly, the silky feel of her dark hair brushing across his hand made him pause. She stared at him, her chocolate brown eyes wide behind the black-rimmed glasses. His gaze fell to her mouth. He could always kiss her the next time she went off on one of her verbal ramblings.

The thought sparked his primitive instincts. He sucked in a breath and jerked his hand away. Yep. Time to go.

Pine Mills High School hadn't changed much in the ten-plus years since Mike wandered its halls. He led Monah to the principal's office where the same secretary sat behind the same weathered desk wearing almost the same green T-shirt emblazoned with the school's mascot. She directed them to the superintendent's office then went back to typing.

"*Pssst!* Mike. Hey, Mike." Monah beckoned to him from the hallway.

Mike glanced up then shook his head. The girl could scoot when she wanted to. He moved to join her. "What is it?"

"Down there." She pointed past a long row of lockers to a classroom. The door stood slightly ajar. "Isn't that Miss Tait's room?"

That was strange. Weren't all the teachers supposed to be on break? So who was in Miss Tait's room in the middle of summer? Drawn in spite of himself, Mike tipped his head toward Monah and dropped his voice to match her whisper. "There's a light on."

"I know. Who do you suppose is in there?"

"Is there something else I can do for you folks?"

They jumped guiltily. Glaring over her glasses at them, the secretary sat with her curled hands hovering above the keyboard.

"Uh"—straightening his shoulders, Mike shrugged into his policeman's demeanor—"the classroom down the hall. Can you tell me who—?"

"The janitor."

"Oh. Right."

She speared him with her gaze. "Anything else?"

"That's it. We appreciate your help." He eased from the entrance before she could ask for his tardy pass. Funny how walking into this building sent him back ten years. "Thanks a lot, Monah," he said, taking her arm and leading her in the direction of the superintendent's office.

"What'd I do?"

"You got me in trouble."

"Your fault. You should have smiled at her."

"Like that would've helped."

"It would've swayed me."

"Oh really?" Charmed by her infectious teasing, he caught her hand and pulled her around in front of him.

She smiled up at him. "Uh-huh."

How long had it been since they'd spent time together? Too long. Not since fires started cropping up all over town. Much as he enjoyed the flirtatious banter, Mike quelled the desire to keep it going and pressed his finger to the tip of her nose. "I'll have to remember that."

To his delight, she looked disappointed when he moved away and pushed open the door that led to the superintendent's hall. After a short bit of looking, they found the engraved plate the secretary told them would lead to his office and let themselves inside.

A young receptionist, her desk covered with photos of two small children, greeted them. "Can I help you?"

Flashing his badge would ensure they got prompt attention, but they weren't here on official business. Instead, Mike pulled a business card from his wallet and presented it to her. "We're here to see Dr. Randolf."

The woman glanced at the card. "Was he expecting you?"

"Not exactly. We were hoping we'd catch him in."

"Ah." The receptionist nodded. "I'm very sorry, but Dr. Randolf is vacationing in Hawaii. I can let you speak to his secretary if you'd like. Perhaps she can schedule an appointment."

Monah's face fell in a frown. She glanced up at him. "What do you think?"

Mike shrugged. "Better than nothing." After she nodded in agreement, Mike signaled to the receptionist, and he and Monah sat down to wait. A moment later, a tall woman dressed in a pale gray pantsuit appeared. Mike guessed her to be in her late forties or early fifties, obviously in shape and attractive by any standard.

She extended her hand, shook his first and then Monah's. "Good afternoon, Detective Brockman. I'm Ms. Wallace. Hailey"—she gestured to the receptionist—"tells me you wanted to speak to Dr. Randolf?"

"That's correct. I understand he's out of town?" Mike said.

"Unfortunately." She smiled, her gaze holding his a fraction of a second too long. "Why don't you come back to my office, and we'll see if there's something I can help you with."

Mike glanced at Monah. Oh yeah, she felt it, too. Her face looked chiseled from stone. Better get in and out of here fast. He moved aside to let Monah precede him as they followed Ms. Wallace down the hall.

The office she led them into could have been cut from a magazine. Ornate paintings decorated the walls, and cinnamon wafted from a scented oil pot. Missing were the pictures that had dotted the receptionist's desk. No kids. No wedding photo. Not even a Polaroid of Ms. Wallace herself.

She gestured toward two gleaming leather chairs opposite her desk. Mike took one, Monah the other.

Mike began, "You see, Ms. Wallace—"

"Simone."

He lifted an eyebrow. "Excuse me?"

"You may call me Simone."

"Yes." He cleared his throat and avoided looking at Monah. He could feel the heat from her glare already. "You see, Simone, my girlfriend, Monah, and I were wondering if it would be possible to get copies of the minutes from the last few board meetings. I understand they are a matter of public record."

Score with the "my girlfriend and I." Monah relaxed, and so did he.

Simone's blue gaze swung to rest on Monah. He tensed, but for once, Monah remained silent. Simone heaved a sigh. "Yes, that's correct. Is there something in particular you're looking for?"

Mike shook his head. "We're not sure, exactly. Perhaps a list of people who addressed the board?"

Interest flickered in Simone's gaze. She leaned back in her chair and folded her arms. "People address the board all the time, Detective." She lifted a slender eyebrow. "May I call you Mike?"

Subtract two points. Monah bristled again. He cleared his throat. "Mike is fine. You say it's not uncommon for people to speak before the board?"

Simone waved her hand. "Complaints against the coaches mostly, but every now and then, something unusual pops up. How far back did you want to go?"

"Several months, if possible."

"Oh, it's possible. It just may take a little time." She turned to the computer on her desk, paused before actually touching the keyboard, and looked at Monah. "Would you like something to drink while I do this?"

Mike didn't doubt Monah was thirsty. She'd talked almost nonstop since they left the library.

"A Coke might be nice," Monah said, with the first hint of a smile since Simone appeared.

A very broad, very satisfied smirk creased Simone's red lips. "Down the hall, first door on your left. Cokes are in the fridge, ice is in the door."

Mike wanted to smack his forehead on the desk. Instead, he jumped to his feet. "I'll get it."

"Don't bother," Monah said, her voice frosty. She strode out the door.

Mentally groaning, Mike plopped back into his seat. He'd pay for that later, and it wasn't even his fault.

"Girlfriend, huh? Too bad. The good ones are always taken." Simone propped her elbows on the desk then rested her chin on her laced fingers. "So tell me again what you need."

The room suddenly felt much too small. Mike straightened, tried to push his chair back another couple of inches, and finally spoke. "Board reports from the last six months or so."

"Is that all? You'd have to go a lot further than that to find anything really worth reading."

Intrigued by the secretive gleam in her eyes, he risked a peek over his shoulder—no sign of Monah—then shifted forward. "Is that right?"

"Uh-huh. You interested?"

"I might be."

Her eyes sparkled with delight. She drew the keyboard toward her, tapped a few keys, and then hit PRINT. Whirring softly, the laser printer spit out several sheets of paper in rapid succession. She collected them, then slid something from a drawer in her desk and added it to the stack.

"Don't tell anyone where you got that last one," she purred, her hand lingering on his as she passed him the pages.

Mike rose, trying hard to pull his hand away without appearing too obvious. "I won't. Thanks, Ms. Wa—" Her brows lowered in disapproval. "Simone."

He beat it to the door before things got more uncomfortable. Monah waited in the hall, her back resting against the painted brick, arms crossed.

"Finished already?"

"Yeah."

"Got everything you *need*?"

So she'd heard that. Mike grabbed her hand and gave it a squeeze. "Right here. Let's go." He pulled her to the parking lot, deposited her inside his car, and then scrambled to the driver's side, itching to see what Simone had taken such pains to include.

Once inside, he flipped over the top sheet of paper and scanned the words.

Monah grabbed her seat belt, slid it across her body, and clicked it into place. "What is that?"

Mike checked the date on the document then read over it again.

"Mike?"

He lifted his head. "I'm not sure. Ms. Wallace gave it to me."

"Let me see it."

He passed it to her. When she finished, she looked at him. "This thing is twenty years old. Apart from the regular business—purchases certain members are pushing the school district to make, resignations, and such—all it says is that Miss Tait addressed the board. So what?" She handed the sheet back to him. "What's so important about that?"

"I don't know, but I think. . ." He paused to peer into her eyes.

She lowered her chin and drew back, her eyes suspicious. "What?"

"You're not going to like it."

"Like what?"

"I think we have to visit with Ms. Wallace again."

CHAPTER EIGHT

I'm gonna have to hurt him.

Monah's fingers tightened on the strap of her seat belt. She took a deep breath, licked her lips, and formed her words carefully. "Go back in?"

Mike avoided her gaze and nodded. Yes, she'd have to strangle him.

"To talk to the secretary?"

Again he nodded, this time with a shrug thrown in.

I'll hog-tie him and drag him away—anything to keep him from walking back into the clutches of that flirty Simone Wallace. Jealousy had nothing to do with it. Monah was only looking out for their forthcoming marriage and the children who would follow. Okay, so he hadn't even proposed yet. She was looking out for that, too. Ms. Wallace may have longer fingernails, but Monah was sure she could take her. She knew martial arts almost as well as the fictional crime-fighting detective Brandy Purcell, or at least well enough to—

"Monah?"

She pushed up her glasses and focused on Mike's face. "Yes?"

"Did you hear what I said?"

Of course not. She was busy protecting their future. "What?"

He tilted his head and cocked an eyebrow. "What were you

just think—? Never mind. I probably don't want to know." He turned in the seat. "I said going back in to question Ms. Wallace is the only way we'll find out what she meant."

"About what?"

Mike ran his finger along the inside of his collar then loosened his tie and released the top button. She didn't feel a bit sorry for him. He deserved to be uncomfortable after that flirting episode. "Ah, after you stepped out, Ms. Wallace insinuated there was something worth reading about this particular meeting." He tapped the paper. "Since it has Miss Tait's name listed, it has to have something to do with her. This might be just the information we need."

She sat back and crossed her arms. Were men really that blind to the wiles of women?

"Did you happen to wonder why she didn't give you the rest of the minutes for that meeting?"

"Huh?" He scanned the sheet, flipped it over and back again. "You don't think this is all of it?"

Oh wow. He really didn't get it. "She only gave you that much of it so you'd have to return for the rest."

Mike's jaw dropped and then slammed closed again. "I guess it worked, didn't it?"

The timid smile that followed made her want to laugh and groan at the same time. "I'll go back in and get the rest." She patted his hand and released her seat belt. "You stay here and file this experience into your memory bank of life lessons."

"But what if—"

She put her fingers over his lips. "Trust me. I know how to handle this situation."

He locked hold of her fingers and kept them in place long enough to place a kiss on the tips. The edges of her heart turned up with the corners of her mouth.

"I'll be right back."

She yanked on the handle and gave the door a shove. Before she could step out, a car barreled into the parking lot. The suggestion that Mike give the maniac a ticket caught in her throat as she recognized Mr. Dyer behind the wheel. He looked angry, a cell phone pressed to his ear as he sped by. She pulled the door closed. Maybe he wouldn't see them.

"Look at that idiot," Mike growled. "Doesn't that guy realize there could be children walking around?"

Thoughts spun in Monah's head almost as fast as Dyer's wheels. "Do you know who that is? That's Greg Dyer, Paul Dyer's father."

Mike peered out the windshield. "So?"

Leaning over slowly to keep from drawing Mr. Dyer's attention, Monah tapped Mike's arm but kept her eyes on Dyer.

"Good grief, Monah. My dog can't scratch his fleas as fast as you're patting my arm."

She gasped as she spun toward him. "I can't believe you just compared me to a dog."

Mike's mouth bobbed open and closed. "He's a really smart dog." He grinned.

If he wasn't so stinking handsome... "I guess that's something." She fought a smile and lost, then turned to see what Mr. Dyer was up to. He disappeared through the main doors. Monah itched to follow. "Did you see the way he raced inside? Let's go see what he's doing here."

"Wait."

"Why? He's got a head start on us as it is."

She unlatched the door, but Mike pulled her back in and held her. "Going in right now might not be a good idea."

She stared. Surely he wasn't serious. "How else are we going to find out why he's here?"

"We wait until he leaves."

"What? Mike, to catch him in the act—"

"Of what? Checking on Paul's grades? There could be any number of reasons he stopped by the school. He is on the board, you know. He might be here on business."

Monah crossed her arms. "Yeah, and that's the business we need to know about. Look at all the evidence against him so far." She held out one finger. "He was in the library the day Miss Tait died." A second finger popped up. "I saw him trying to give her some money, probably a bribe." She put up a third finger. "He and Paul came to the library looking for Miss Tait's papers. If you ask me, that means anything he does at this school should be deemed highly suspicious."

Mike smiled and grasped her three fingers in his hands. "Don't you think if he was here to do something illegal, he'd stop the moment he saw us?"

Rats. He had a point. But maybe. . .

"If I go in by myself, he won't be as leery as if he saw you."

"And what reason would you give him for being here?"

Mike's phone rang before she could come up with a good answer.

"Detective Brockman here."

Monah had to smile. He sounded so cool and professional. Nothing like the way he talked to her.

"All right. I'm on my way."

No! They couldn't leave now. They were so close to obtaining a clue to Miss Tait's death.

"We've got to go."

"But, Mike—"

"Sorry, Monah. Duty calls. I'll come back another time to get the rest of the minutes and use that as an excuse to ask about Dyer."

Over her dead body. Simone would enjoy having him to herself way too much.

"Just leave me here."

Mike sighed. "Look at the time, Monah. They're about to close up. Besides, how will you get back to the library?" He started the car. "Buckle up."

Well, if this wasn't the worst cliffhanger she'd ever seen. This whole clue hunt didn't go at all as she'd pictured. She slammed the door and latched her seat belt. She'd have to think of another way. But just in case. . .

"You'll let me know what you find out, won't you?"

He kept his eyes straight ahead. "I can't say. It depends on how it fits in with my investigation. I'll tell you what I can."

If that didn't beat all. It was her idea to come here in the first place. Well, she'd just keep up her own investigation. She'd gotten pretty good at research, which would serve her well with this murder case. Nothing like a mystery to get the juices flowing.

~

"Here you go, Detective. Coffee, strong and black, just how you like it."

Mike looked up and smiled at Lucy, Pine Mills Deli's only waitress. "Thanks, Lucy. I appreciate the effort, but you really didn't have to bother brewing a fresh pot."

"No bother for one of Pine Mills's finest." Lucy shifted to rest her hip against a corner of the booth. "So, how's the investigation going?"

"What investigation?"

Lucy gave a throaty chuckle, her voice roughened by years of smoking. "Don't try and pull one over on me, Detective. I see who your company is." She gestured to the door where Ted Levy was just making his way inside.

Mike laughed and shook his head. "Nothing gets past you, Luce. Might as well bring another coffee. Ted and I will probably be here awhile."

While she shuffled off to do his bidding, Ted joined him in the booth.

"Thanks for meeting me here," Mike said. "You know how I hate your 'office.'"

"Almost as much as I hate yours."

The familiar joke still brought a grin. Mike pushed the creamer and sweetener packets toward Ted, knowing he'd need them. "What've you got for me?"

Ted tipped his head to a spot just over Mike's shoulder. A moment later, Lucy set down his coffee and a carafe for refills.

"Anything else I can do for you boys?"

Mike handed her a five-dollar bill. "That'll about do it. Thanks, Lucy."

The money quickly disappeared into her apron pocket. "Let me know if you change your mind."

Her shoes whooshed softly across the checkered floor as she crossed to a table littered with the remains of someone's lunch. She wouldn't bother them again. That's why Mike liked this place. Lucy was discreet. He turned to Ted. "So?"

The buckles on Ted's briefcase snapped open. He pulled a folder out and slid it across the table. "Take a look."

"The toxicology report?"

"Uh-huh."

"That was quick."

"I called in a favor."

Mike spent a couple of minutes skimming the findings. When he finished, he pointed to a word midway down the page. "*Aconi. . .tum* what?"

"*Aconitum noveboracense,*" Ted said. "Better known as monkshood."

"Monkshood." Mike rolled the word around in his mouth.

Emptying a creamer packet into his coffee, Ted stirred thoughtfully. "Wolfsbane, friar's cap, mourning bride. . .same thing."

Mike gave a slow nod. Wolfsbane he'd heard before. "Unbelievable. She was poisoned by something out of Merlin's medicine cabinet."

"I wouldn't go that far." Ted took a sip from his cup. He grimaced and reached for a second creamer packet. "Monkshood is not all that hard to come by, what with its unusual blooms. People plant it in their gardens all over Europe."

A thick blanket of discouragement settled over Mike's shoulders. "Which means just about anybody could have murdered Charlotte Tait."

Ted shrugged. "Sorry, pal. At least now you have your murder weapon."

"Not exactly. Do we know how the killer got the poison into her system?"

"Could've happened any number of ways—ingested through something she ate, topical application in cosmetics or perfume"—he lifted an eyebrow—"you name it. Monkshood is pretty potent stuff, so depending on the solution, it wouldn't necessarily take much to be fatal."

"But it wasn't through the water she drank."

Ted shook his head. "Nope. That stuff was clean."

Mike leaned back in the booth. "And that puts me firmly

back at square one."

A bronze bell above the entry jingled merrily. From the corner of his eye, Mike recognized Wayne Drolen. The woman on his arm was anyone but his wife. Mike shot a glance at Ted. "Know her?"

Ted shook his head. "I know of her. She's the publicist Wayne hired to help him promote the new sports facility he wants to build."

Mike eyed the sultry blond. Her snug skirt and heavy makeup left little doubt in his mind what she was hoping to promote. She leaned into Drolen, her lips curved in a pouty smile, her gaze warm and inviting as she stared into his face. Mike wrapped his fingers around the rim of his cup. "I wonder if that's all she is."

The couple wound their way to a table snuggled into a corner of the deli. Hand lifted, Drolen gestured for the female to sit, his fingers resting lightly on her bare shoulder as he held her chair. Ted twisted to peer at them over the top of his seat. With their backs to him, neither Wayne nor the woman noticed. Giving a grunt, Ted turned back around. "That guy's all bluff. He likes to flirt, and the ladies find him attractive, but he's way too worried about his reputation on the city council to risk an affair."

Mike wasn't so certain. A niggling suspicion formed in his brain. "What if this time he messed up? If a rival for the funds donated to the city found out about it. . ."

Just how far would Drolen go to cover up his indiscretions? He read the answer in the troubled lines of Ted's brow.

CHAPTER NINE

Monah flopped onto the chair behind the counter. There weren't many days she didn't want to be at the library. Unfortunately, this was one of them. Monday was supposed to be her day off. Of all the times for Sandy to have a doctor's appointment. Now Casey would have all the fun following up on suspects. Envy spun through Monah like a revolving door.

Groaning, she forced herself to stop drumming her fingers on the counter and ignored the intense desire to call Casey. Instead, she grabbed the top book off the stack to give her hands something to do. It was either that or go over and scold Scott and Tony for getting too loud, and in her current mood, she might come across as a grouch. Besides, if she phoned again, her friend might stop by just to kill her. A quick glance at the clock told her it had been only fifteen minutes since her last call. She'd have to behave herself and wait another fifteen.

Her attitude wasn't her fault. She blamed Mike. Except for the brief hour they sat together at church, he'd left her on her own all weekend. He could have at least appeased her curiosity by—

Spotting one of her favorite customers headed her way, Monah put on her brightest smile. "Good morning, Mrs. Sparks. Did Mom send you to spy on me, or is there something I can help you with?"

The elderly woman chuckled and shook her bony finger. "You mean to tell me there's a need to be spying? Shame on you."

Monah held up both hands. "Now, now. You know I'm the most innocent girl in town." She stepped around the counter and gave her mother's neighbor a hug. As usual, the faint scent of mothballs drifted to her nose. "What can I do for you?"

"I can't find that gardening book I borrowed last year." She rubbed her arms. "I stopped looking, though, when I got cold. You having trouble with your air conditioner again, dear? It's a mite cool, don't you think?"

"Is it really?" Monah thought it felt fine, but she had been rather preoccupied thinking about Casey. She hoped the sweet woman wasn't getting sick. Then again, Mrs. Sparks didn't have a spare ounce of flesh to help keep her warm. "Let me get you my sweater."

"Oh no." Mrs. Sparks grasped Monah's hand. "Don't bother. I decided I'm going to visit that handsome landscaper, Luke Kerrigan. He can answer all my questions. Besides, if I get home too soon, Clarence will still be working in the garden." She pulled Monah close. "You know how the two of us can't be in there at the same time."

Monah grinned. She'd witnessed plenty growing up, and now her mother kept her filled in on their shenanigans. There wasn't a more loving couple in town until they tried to garden together. Their last name well described the results.

Mrs. Sparks reared her head back and peered at Monah through her bifocals. "You know what that man had the nerve to call my brand of fertilizer? Snake oil. Can you believe that? Why, it's the best on the market. All his stuff does is burn the plants till they die. If it weren't for my abilities, we'd not eat a bite of produce. And the flowers? I bet if those poor things could pull themselves up by the roots and move out, they would."

Monah clapped her hand over her mouth to keep from laughing out loud. She leaned in and whispered, "I guess it does no good to tell him to stay out."

"Are you kidding? He doesn't think I have a blessed brain cell left in my head where gardening is concerned." She gave a woeful shake of her head. "He nearly drives me batty when he pulls out his knife to see if the seeds have germinated. I just know he's going to accidentally kill them. Half the time, I think he shows me his knife just to get me riled." She patted Monah's hand. "Oh, don't get me started, or I'll go on and on."

As if she hadn't already. Monah loved the dear woman like a second mother, but she sure could be a chatty old soul. "You sure you don't want something to keep you warm? I'll help you find that book." She moved behind the counter and scanned the shelves. She was sure she'd left the sweater where she could reach it. Sandy must have moved it. "Do you remember the title?"

"No, that was much too long ago. The cover had a whole bunch of flowers on it, though."

Monah looked over her glasses at her. Was she serious? Most gardening books had flowers on the cover.

Mrs. Sparks laughed and waved her hand as she tottered to the door. "Don't worry yourself, dear. I'll ask Luke my questions."

"All right. Tell Mr. Sparks hello for me."

Mike entered behind a flock of chatty patrons. Even when she was upset with him, he still had the ability to make her heart pound. Maybe he'd come by to reschedule their movie date. Or maybe he planned to fill her in on his investigation of Miss Tait's death. Either one would make her day.

The look of surprise on his face did nothing for her morale.

"Monah? What are you doing here? I thought you had Monday off."

Her heart sank. Was that why he chose today to come in? "Sandy had an appointment. When she returns, I'll get to leave."

He smiled. "Suits me just fine. I can't think of a better librarian to assist me."

He was here on business. She'd be helping him. Things were looking up. "How can I help?"

"Two things." He glanced around then angled his way behind the counter, his back to the patrons. "I need to see all the books you have on poison, and I need to know who checked them out in the last few months."

The news slammed into Monah's stomach. "So she really was killed after all." Swallowing didn't help the lump in her throat. The information also moved her mind into high gear. "What kind of poison?"

"Now, Monah—"

"I'm not being nosy." At his raised eyebrows, she backpedaled. "Well, kind of, but knowing exactly what to look for will cut down on wasted time and effort." That sounded convincing, didn't it? His bland expression said otherwise.

"Monah, I need to see *all* nonfiction books about poison. If I need something more detailed, I'll ask."

Talk about dangling a piece of chocolate only to yank it away. How cruel could he be? "All right. Give me a few minutes to find the references. You can start locating them while I check to see if any of them have been borrowed."

She typed in the keywords then printed off the list and handed it to him. "Start in that section right over there." She pointed toward an aisle near the restrooms. "I'll be with you in a few minutes."

Monah did a search for the names of people who had last borrowed the poison books. Two names popped up. Shock ricocheted through her system. She dropped onto the stool and peered in Mike's direction, then headed his way to see if he'd have the same reaction.

She found him thumbing through one of the books. Several lay open at his feet. Curious, she stepped closer and tried to read the section titles.

"Monah."

She jerked back a step. Caught. She opened her eyes wide and batted her lashes a few times. "Yes?" He probably wouldn't buy the innocent act, but she had to try.

He grinned and shook his head. She waited for him to continue. He only stood there staring at the book in his hands. He ran his finger over part of a page. What was so interesting in that book? She moved a bit closer and tilted her head. He slammed it shut, making her jump.

"Did anyone check out these books lately?"

"Two names came up."

A shadow fell across the aisle. "Excuse me. Monah?"

Jamie hovered nearby, her eyes glued to the books on the floor. To keep her from seeing too much, Monah led her away. "Is something wrong?"

"No. Sandy just wanted me to let you know she's back."

Monah peeked over Jamie's shoulder and returned Sandy's wave. "Good. Thanks, Jamie."

"Does this mean I can go to lunch now?"

Monah glanced at the clock. "It's not even eleven yet. Can you wait awhile longer?" At her nod, Monah gestured to the back. "Check with Sandy before you go. I'm going to help the detective a bit more and then I'll be leaving."

Jamie walked away looking. . .what? Nervous? Scared? Monah retraced her steps to Mike. She hoped Jamie didn't plan on quitting. They needed the help this summer.

"Anything wrong?" He quirked an eyebrow.

"Nope. She just let me know Sandy's back."

"Good. So what names did you pull up?"

Back to business. "You'll never believe it." She edged to his side to keep anyone from overhearing. "Lauren Beck and Ms. Wallace."

He leaned back. "Simone?"

Hackles on full alert, Monah's hands went to her hips. "You're on a first-name basis with her?"

Mike laughed. "Relax, Monah. I just wanted to make sure we're talking about the same woman."

Gradually, she relented. "Okay."

As much as she'd love to pin everything on that woman, she had to let Mike know her thoughts. "I've been thinking. We've been centering our attention on those who were in the library at the time of Miss Tait's death."

"Yeah."

"Well, since it was poison that killed her, it really could have been anyone, not just those here that afternoon. Poison sometimes takes hours to work, depending on type and dosage."

Mike nodded. "You're right. We need to add the names of anyone who saw her that day."

His use of "we" warmed her again. "Right. And another thing, anyone could have read these books to get the information they wanted. People sometimes spend hours in here. They don't need to check the books out to get what they want. Not only that, but anyone with Internet access can find this same information."

Mike frowned. "I know. That thought crossed my mind earlier, but I still had to look. Sure makes my job harder. Sometimes I hate the Internet." He bent to close the books on the floor. "I need to take these with me."

She squatted to help him. "That's fine. Just let me check them out for you." She led the way to the counter. "What's your next step?" He didn't speak right away. His expression let her know he heard but didn't want to answer. "You're going back to the school, aren't you?"

"Monah—"

"I'm going with you." Where exactly did people find a No TRESPASSING sign?

"You can't."

"I can either ride with you or follow you."

"I'm in the middle of an investigation. I have to go alone."

She clenched her teeth to keep from arguing. Whether he liked it or not, she would get to that school. He may not appreciate it now, but he'd thank her after she finished running interference against that conniving secretary.

CHAPTER TEN

Mike shifted the books in his arms so they rested on his hip. Now that he had the information he needed, he could focus on more pleasant things. Much more pleasant.

His breath caught as Monah lifted her chin and stared at him, her eyes flashing. When she looked at him like that, all fiery and possessive, it was all he could do not to sweep her into his arms and kiss her.

He leaned forward, close enough so that the clean, natural scent of her delicate perfume tantalized his senses. "You have nothing to worry about, you know." His voice dropped to a whisper. "The longer I'm with you, the more certain I am you're the only woman for me."

Her soft intake of breath left him reeling, a feeling he was fast becoming accustomed to. Instead of lessening over time as he'd expected, it seemed to grow stronger.

"What are you doing over the Fourth of July?" The question popped out before he could think, before he could remember what he'd meant to ask.

The bemused look cleared from her smoky eyes. "What?"

Mike drew back, creating space so he could think clearly. "The fire department fund-raiser. I'm manning a booth. I've been meaning to ask if you'd like to come with me—maybe help out— but it kept slipping my mind."

As quickly as it appeared, the smile fled from Monah's face. "I—I—"

"We can pack a picnic basket and have lunch in the park." Teasing, he leaned toward her. "If you're really good, I'll even treat you to my famous fried chicken."

Monah blinked. "You cook?"

"Mom's recipe." He laughed at her crestfallen expression. "We don't have to have chicken. I can make sandwiches instead."

"No, it's not that." She reached under the counter and pulled out a fluorescent yellow flyer.

He scanned the words then lifted an eyebrow. "A book sale fund-raiser?"

She pointed glumly to several large boxes of books stacked near the windows. "Sandy and Jamie worked on them all weekend. We're sorting through the older things, getting them ready to sell. Afterward, we'll use the profits to update the shelves with newer stuff."

Disappointment flashed through him but only for a second. He grinned and grasped her hand in a quick squeeze. "No problem. You still have to eat, right? Just name the time and place. I'll bring it all. You won't have to worry about a thing."

"But—"

"No buts. It's not like I won't be able to find you in the booming metropolis of Pine Mills." Mike laughed and gathered the books back into his arms. "I'll call you."

She nodded, and Mike left the library, a spring in his step. Maybe this whole investigation thing wouldn't be so bad. He liked knowing that Monah cared enough to be jealous.

Tossing the stack of books onto the backseat of his car, Mike once again spied the cover on the thickest of the bunch. *Medicinal Plants and Herbs.* A sliver of foreboding crept into his gut. Several times throughout its pages, words and phrases were circled. He'd have a lot of research to do once he got back to the station, and he wasn't all that certain he'd like what he found.

The drive back to the school lasted just long enough to create worry in Mike's head. If the circled words were tied to the poison used to kill Miss Tait, what would that mean for Monah? A deeper, more thorough search of the library? Her testimony, assuming they were ever able to bring the case to court? He refused to consider any other options.

Like the last time, very few people traversed the halls of Pine Mills High School. Mike skipped the principal's office and went straight to the receptionist at the superintendent's office.

"Ms. Wallace?" The young receptionist shook her head. "I'm sorry, sir. She's out until Thursday. Some fancy conference she goes to every year up around Marlborough."

Mike glanced at the board minutes in his hand. Great. She hadn't mentioned she'd be unavailable the last time he was here. Impatience plucked at his nerves. "Thursday, you say? Any chance you'll be hearing from her before then?"

The girl gave a sympathetic shake of her head. "Not really. Those ladies are really into their stuff. Simone rants about the trip for weeks leading up to the conference." Her gaze brightened. "We've got a sub in for her though. Would you like to speak to her?"

Couldn't hurt. Mike nodded and sat down to wait. Within minutes, he was following the slender, dark-haired replacement into Simone Wallace's immaculate office.

The woman gestured to a chair before seating herself behind the desk. "I'm sorry, sir. What did you say your name is again?"

"Mike Brockman. I'm a detective with PMPD."

"Pleasure to meet you, Detective. I'm Regina Smith. What

can I help you with today?"

A large vase of freshly cut blooms crowded one corner of the desk. Mike leaned forward to get a better view of Miss Smith's face.

"Here, let me move those," she said, smiling as she picked up the vase and set it on the table behind her. "Simone left them. I just enjoy looking at them. She always has such good taste."

"She does," Mike agreed with a quick glance around the room. Maybe it was the gardening books he'd spent all morning studying or perhaps Ted Levy's words ringing in his head. Whatever the cause, for the first time, Mike noticed just how many of the pictures scattered on the walls had to do with plants. "She must really like flowers."

"Loves 'em." Miss Smith nodded. "So what can I do for you?"

Changing his mind in an instant, Mike tucked the minutes into the pocket of his jacket. "Tell you what. I'll just stop by another time to see Dr. Randolf."

"Okay. Anything else I can help you with, Detective?"

"That'll be all." Mike rose and shook the woman's hand. "Thanks for your time."

Her pleasant smile was still in place when he glanced back from the door. Before he ducked out of the building, he stopped by the receptionist's desk.

She looked up from a stack of invoices she was sorting. "Yes, sir?"

Mike shoved one hand into his pocket. "Ms. Wallace—what kind of conference did you say she went to?"

The frown cleared from the receptionist's face. "Some garden-club thing—Massachusetts Horticulture Society, I think she called it."

The name pounded in Mike's head all the way to his car.

Simone Wallace was attending a meeting of the Horticulture Society, and that meant she was probably very knowledgeable about plants.

"I take it the substitute wasn't much help?"

Mike jerked his head up at the sound of Monah's voice. "What are you doing here?"

"Protecting my investment." Instead of explaining the puzzling words, she circled his car and stepped into his hug. "So? Nothing?"

Mike hesitated, only for a split second but long enough to raise her suspicions.

"You did learn something!"

He shook his head and tightened his hold on her waist. "Just a hunch, and not something I can talk about."

"Ah, I see. I guess you wouldn't be interested in anything I found out either then."

He frowned. "Something at the library?"

She pulled from his arms, a secretive grin tugging at her lips. "Uh-uh."

"Casey?"

"Nope. Something I learned here."

His stomach sank. She'd been investigating on her own? That explained the investment comment. She was protecting herself and the library. "Monah—"

"Simone loves plants. She's at a meeting of the Horticulture Society in Marlborough. I asked the receptionist when I went inside." Her words came faster, with rising urgency. "That's suspicious, don't you think, especially since the weapon used against Miss Tait was likely some kind of readily available poison? I bet if we searched her house—"

"Whoa." Mike put up his hand to stop her. "Nobody's

searching Simone Wallace's house based on a hunch, especially without a warrant."

Her eyes narrowed. "Wait. . .so you already knew?"

Mike stopped short. "What?"

"You've actually thought about a warrant, which means the hunch you mentioned earlier was about Simone?"

How did she always do that? How did she get things out of him even when he was careful to be on his guard? "I didn't say that."

She gave a knowing nod. "Okay, Detective Brockman. If that's how you want to play it." She took a sheet of paper from her purse.

"What's that?"

"Something I thought you might be interested in."

Mike glanced at the heading typed in bold print across the top: DEADLY DOSES: A WRITER'S GUIDE TO POISONS.

Her head dipped like a bobber on the water. "The source I used to find out exactly how monkshood works and what the side affects are." She pointed at the paper. "I printed them off for you."

"You—you—," Mike sputtered.

Monah pulled a second item from her purse, a small book stamped with the library address. "This was in the box of older stuff we plan to sell. That's why it wasn't on the list I gave you. Sandy had already removed it from our active files."

Plants That Poison. Mike grimaced at the title. He didn't need to look inside the cover to guess what had tipped Monah off to which poison had killed Miss Tait. "I take it you found the circled words?"

She nodded. "What do you think it means?"

"It means," Mike said, sighing, "the Pine Mills Police Department has another full-fledged murder case on its hands."

CHAPTER ELEVEN

Another murderer in Pine Mills.

The whole idea sent chills through Monah. She drove away from her house wishing she could just as easily escape her troubled thoughts. Under better circumstances, she'd be on her way to the city council meeting to face off against Miss Tait for the donated funds. Tonight the meeting would take place with one less citizen. What was her small town coming to? She used to feel so safe. Now even the elderly were targets.

The majority of the day, Monah and Casey researched monkshood. Not an easy task since Mike had taken all the reference books. Monah was thankful she had her laptop. They scouted the Internet until they learned more about the plant than they cared to know. Basically, most anyone in the northern states could grow the stuff.

Once Casey saw a picture of the plant, she recalled seeing the same thing growing in Aunt Liddy's garden. A quick phone call later, and they discovered that all the people in her garden club had received seeds last year. From what Aunt Liddy told them, most of her friends were members of the club, Monah's mom included. She could still hear Mike's moan when she told him the news.

The tune to "Mama Said (There'd Be Days Like This)" played

on her cell phone. She pulled the phone from her purse and flipped it open.

"Hi, Mom."

"I couldn't stop thinking of you, dear. I had to call and make sure you were all right."

Monah smiled. Her mother hadn't given birth to her, but she was still the best mom in the world. "I'm fine."

"Not nervous?"

"I didn't say that." The two shared a laugh. "I've been trying to think of anything but what I'm up against tonight."

"You really think it'll be that bad? I mean, Miss Tait, um. . ."

Poor Mom. Couldn't even speak the words. "I know what you're saying, but I still have to deal with Wayne Drolen. He's already a huge step ahead of me just because he's a councilman. They're bound to favor him."

The silence on the other end spoke volumes. Her mother agreed. Monah's heart sank a little lower. Fighting for the donated funds wasn't a struggle she cherished, but since she believed so strongly in the library's need for computers, she'd put on her armor and go to battle.

"Speak from your heart, Monah. Let them see your passion, that you're a woman of integrity. You'd be surprised how that might move them toward your side."

If only that were so. "I just wish everyone loved the library as much as I do. But you know, I bet there are some who've lived in this town for years and never set foot inside the building."

A soft chuckle sounded on the other end. "Well now, dear. Don't use that as a defense, or you'll never get any funding."

Monah laughed at the gentle chiding in her mother's voice. "You're probably right. I'll leave that part out when I state my case."

"Good idea. You know I'd be there if I could."

"I know. But Dad will be home soon, and he can't manage without you."

Another chuckle followed her soft groan. "Maybe someday I'll get him raised."

Monah easily pictured the tender smile on her mother's face as she peered out the living room window seeking her true love's car. Monah hoped that one day she'd be doing the same thing.

"I'll be praying for you."

Her mom's words brought her back to real life. "Thanks. I'll need it. I'll let you know how it goes."

Monah pushed the END button as she pulled up to the one stoplight in Pine Mills. Ken Greer drove through the intersection, a cocky grin on his face, his hand raised in a two-fingered salute. Without a doubt, he was headed to the same meeting to beg for the same money.

She turned the corner and trailed him down the street into the city hall parking lot. Casey's car wasn't among those already parked. Her friend said she'd come for moral support. Monah figured she'd need all the backing she could get. She was probably the least confrontational person in town. The idea of standing up in front of even a small number of people turned her stomach into one large acid pit.

Praying that Casey would get there soon, Monah headed inside, staying as far from Ken as she could. He wasn't a bad sort, but sometimes his humor was a bit more biting than she liked. Tonight she wasn't prepared to deal with his brand of wit.

People milled everywhere, and Monah figured most everyone in town had decided to show up for the showdown. They might not get a gun battle and spilled blood, but for the quiet town of Pine Mills, a heated verbal fight was the next best thing. If nothing else, it'd give them fodder for the gossip mill.

Where was Casey? Monah pulled her phone from her purse and squealed when someone grabbed her arm.

"Sandy!" Monah swatted at her. "Good grief, girl. You about made my heart explode."

Sandy made a poor attempt to hide her laugh. "I knew you were a little nervous, so I thought I'd come and at least hold your hand."

What a sweetheart. "A *little* nervous?" She raised her brows and put her hand to her throat. "If I were any more tense, you could pop me with a pin."

"Oh, don't be silly. You'll be fine."

Monah peered at Sandy over the rim of her glasses. "Easy for you to say. You're not the one up there getting skewered and grilled."

Sandy grinned. "You certainly have a way with words." She took Monah's arm and led her toward the chairs. "Come on. Let's get a good seat."

Feet dragging, Monah grudgingly followed. "Doesn't matter which one you put me in. Guaranteed, it'll be hot."

With an outright laugh, Sandy pulled her close. "Monah, you're a hoot. They're gonna love you. They won't be able to help themselves."

If only the council was as easy to please as Sandy. "Whoa." Monah jerked to a stop. "Not so close to the front." Sandy tugged, but Monah stood her ground. "Halfway is close enough."

"All right, but you're going to sit in the aisle chair."

"Why?"

"You're nervous enough as it is. You don't want to climb over a bunch of legs and risk tripping when you go to the front."

What did it matter? She doubted her legs would hold her anyway. "Okay."

She let Sandy in first then plopped onto a chair. Tapping the buttons on her cell phone, Monah bit her lip in consternation. Where was Casey? She attempted to punch in her number but was interrupted by one person after another stopping to say hello or wish her well. Moments later the council members filed in and took their seats.

Mayor Jeff Wright called the meeting to order. Straining awkwardly to punch in Casey's number, Monah squeezed the phone between her and Sandy. Whoever said women glistened instead of sweated didn't know what they were talking about. At the rate she perspired, the custodian would have to bring in a mop right about the time Monah passed out from dehydration.

The phone to her ear, Monah counted the rings. Three. Fo—

"Miss Trenary."

Monah clapped the phone closed. The members of the council, Wayne Drolen included, glared at her. The audience stared and snickered. "Yes?"

The lone female on the board leaned across the table. "Didn't you hear us announce that all cell phones were to be turned off?"

"Oh no. I didn't. Sorry." She slumped back down in her chair and punched the volume button down until it vibrated.

Sandy bumped her with her elbow and leaned close to Monah's ear. "Way to warm them up to you."

How embarrassing. She cast a surreptitious glance around the room. Mike leaned against the far wall. He smiled and nodded. She scrunched a little lower and pressed the heels of her hands against her eyes.

A little help here, Lord?

Maybe Casey came in late and was somewhere behind her. She turned slightly to look. Nothing. Where was she? Monah again held the phone low between her and Sandy and switched to text.

"You're asking for trouble."

Sandy's whisper sent a tremor down her spine. "It'll only take a minute. Keep watch for me."

Monah punched in WHERE R U? and hit the SEND button.

"Miss Trenary."

She slapped the phone closed. The mayor eyed her with disdain.

"It's off. It's off."

Mayor Wright smiled. "We just wanted to know if you still planned to speak during this meeting."

"Oh. Right. Yes, I do."

The mayor grinned. "May everyone addressing the council tonight be as concise as you."

The crowd rumbled with laughter. Oh, to be able to crawl under her chair. This was so not the way she wanted the night to go. She chanced a peek at Mike. Head lowered, he stared at the floor. Was he having second thoughts about her? The vision she had before of waiting and watching for him to get home from work faded.

Sandy bumped her. "You should be studying your notes."

"What notes?"

Sandy's stare said she thought Monah was a complete bone-head. "You didn't write anything down to read as your opening statement?"

She laced her fingers together. "Well, I thought I'd just. . . sort of. . .wing it."

Sandy pursed her lips then forced a smile. "Okay. That's one plan." She pulled a notebook from her bag and pressed it and a pen into Monah's hands. "Another is to write a statement, so if you freeze up at the podium, you can resort to reading."

"Good thinking."

Thankfully, one of the councilmen was droning the minutes

of the last meeting. That meant she'd have plenty of time to get something down. Pen poised over paper, Monah's worst fear happened. No words came. Not a one. Oh, wait. She started scribbling.

"Dear ladies and gentlemen." Nope. Not right. She scratched through 'ladies' and changed it to 'lady,' since only one sat on the council. But even that didn't sound right. She changed it to *"Dear councilmen."* Er, *council people.* Oh, that was terrible. She leaned toward Sandy.

"What should I write?"

Sandy rolled her eyes and took the tablet and pen from her. *Mayor Wright, council members. . .*

Sandy held the tip of the pen under the mayor's name. "Look at him when you address him. Do the same to the others when you say 'council members.' "

"Okay. What else?"

"You've got to let them know how badly the computers with Internet access are needed, that we're extremely behind the times in comparison with other libraries."

Behind them, a short woman with curly brown hair cleared her throat meaningfully.

"Sorry," Monah said, then dropped her voice and tilted her head toward Sandy. "How's the best way to say that?"

Sandy licked her lips and tapped the pen on the notebook. "I'm not sure."

Monah eyed the blank sheet of paper. Words began to trickle then pour through her mind. She grabbed the notebook and pen. "I think I know what to say." All noise and conversations diminished as ideas clamored for attention. She wrote as fast as the ink allowed.

"Well, if it isn't Monah Canary."

The voice speared her in the back of the neck and sliced through every vertebra as it moved down her spine. This was going to be a very bad night.

CHAPTER TWELVE

Compelled to face her high school nemesis, Monah reluctantly turned her head.

Veronica Killion stood with arms crossed, peering down her hawklike nose. "Oh my. Did I accidentally call you 'Canary' again? Sorry."

The snide smile on Veronica's face grated on Monah's nerves. "Hi, Ronnie." Veronica hated that name about as much as Monah disliked Canary.

The smile slid into a sneer. "A little birdie told me you'd be begging for money tonight. Thought I'd come and listen to you twitter."

Monah gritted her teeth. *Be nice. Retract the claws. Christlike attitude. You can do it.* "Well, I hope you enjoy the evening."

"Without a doubt. Ought to be most entertaining. Especially once you get up there."

Monah forced a smile. "I aim to please."

The mayor pounded the gavel. "Can we have some quiet while Wayne is speaking?"

The disruption wasn't her fault. Why was he staring at her instead of Veronica? Face burning, Monah folded her hands and tried to look attentive. From the corner of her eye, she noticed Veronica take a chair not far from the podium. Probably to make sure she was heard when she heckled.

Sandy latched onto her arm. "What's with her?" she hissed into Monah's ear.

"She hates me," Monah said, low enough so as not to attract the mayor's attention.

"I gathered that. Why?"

"She thinks I stole Luke Kerrigan from her back in high school." Did she really have to go into this? Sandy's curious expression said yes. Monah lifted the paper high enough to hide behind. "I used to get picked on a lot. Veronica was the worst. Sometimes I talk a lot and kinda fast when I get nervous."

"No." Lips trembling, she laid her index finger on the side of her face.

"Yes, I do." Then she caught the sarcasm. "Now, Sandy—"

"I'm teasing. Go on."

After a scowl, she continued. "Ronnie got everyone to start calling me 'Canary' instead of Trenary because she said I twittered like a dumb bird."

"Ah. So that's why you're a nervous wreck about getting up there."

She made a face. "Probably has something to do with it."

Sandy pretended to roll up her sleeves. "Ya want I should go mess her up?"

The mafia-type accent made Monah laugh. "Anyway, she used to have a crush on Luke, so when he came to my rescue and stood up for me, Veronica blamed me for losing him." She shook her head. "Some people can't get past their high school hang-ups. You'd think she'd get over this silly feud. Right?"

"You'd think." Sandy scrunched down in her chair, crossed her legs, and scratched at her neck.

Monah eyed her. Why did she suddenly seem so uncomfortable? She peered around to see who might have come in to cause Sandy's discomfort then shrugged it off. If she wanted to finish the speech, she'd better stop wasting time.

After rereading the notes on her pad, she started again.

"Detective Brockman," the mayor said, "you're next. Step to the podium. You'll have three minutes to make a statement. I'll let you know when your time is up."

Monah froze at the mayor's announcement. She snagged Sandy's sleeve and pulled her close. "I thought they'd go over old business first."

"They did. That's what Wayne was talking about."

"Oh great. How am I supposed to write this and listen to Mike at the same time? Worse yet, we only get three minutes? How can I say everything in just three minutes?"

Sandy raised her brows. "You're nervous, remember? You'll probably talk fast enough to get everything said in two."

Monah jabbed Sandy with her elbow. "I can't believe you said that."

"Ladies, please." This time the mayor didn't look a bit amused. "You'll get your turn."

"Sorry." Monah wanted to disappear. Where was a rock when you needed one?

Mike cleared his throat. "Mr. Mayor, council members, I'll keep this brief."

"Thank goodness."

Monah glared at Veronica. That hussy could be rude to her all she liked, but she'd best leave Mike alone if she knew what was good for her. Mike went on as though he hadn't heard. "I've recorded everything in the police station in need of repairs. I've also talked to Andrew Flood with Best Design Construction to get estimates for each renovation."

As Monah listened to Mike read his list, pride for his organizational skills warred with her distinct lack of preparedness.

At least she'd visited or contacted other libraries to find out how much they'd upgraded their systems. She dug through her purse. Relief eased a portion of her discomfort when she spied her findings folded inside the cover of the mininotebook she always carried. After reading through it once, she turned her attention back to Mike just in time to hear him coming to a close.

"There are a few small details I didn't mention that will need to be addressed. All items will bring the total cost to just under half a million dollars. Thank you for your time."

Half a million. That left plenty of funds for the work Monah wanted done at the library. Though they'd mutually agreed it was better that they not discuss the money, she breathed a sigh of relief that their beliefs on how it should be spent wouldn't drive a wedge between them.

The mayor smiled. "Thank you, Detective. If you'll leave a copy of your notes, we'll go over them during our discussions." He nodded toward Ken. "Chief Greer, you're next."

Ken swaggered to the podium in his usual confident style. He addressed the board members by their first names as if they were his best friends. Monah sighed and rolled her eyes. Sure he knew them, but come on.

She honed in on Ken's words. Maybe he'd give her some insight on how to convince the board that the library was worthy of their consideration.

"This town may be small, but that doesn't mean it doesn't deserve the very best in protection. Every citizen has the right to expect a sense of security and the knowledge that rescue will be provided if there's a need."

Ken took a slow turn, looking several of the attendees in the eyes before he faced the board again. "I know for a fact that most of the people here, as well as a good deal of those who couldn't make it tonight, feel a sense of terror at the arsons taking place. I can't help but think that more trucks and men to run them on a full-time basis would ease those fears."

Utter silence filled the room when he paused. Then he slammed his fist on the podium, making everyone jump, Monah included. "I am just one man. I can't do it all. As it stands, we only have volunteers to rely on. It's too much to hope they're not out of town or somehow unavailable to respond when a fire breaks out. The donated funds would be a great start toward paying a full-time staff and adding needed equipment." Leaning forward, he rubbed his hand across the podium, his face solemn. "I'm passionate about protecting my friends. I can only hope you are, too. Thank you."

Monah's chest throbbed with emotion. Ken had her thoroughly convinced every cent should go toward a new fire department, and she didn't need to look around to know others probably felt the same way.

"Miss Trenary, the moment you've waited for has arrived. The floor is yours."

A sharp, stabbing pain started in her head and zipped along her spine to her feet. Pulse racing, she sat up.

Sandy leaned over. "You can do this. Just say what's in your heart."

Monah wanted to laugh. The only thing in her heart at the moment was every ounce of blood in her body fighting for space. There sure couldn't be any in her head, because it felt much too light. She wobbled to her feet and shuffled to the front. Now she knew why Ken grabbed both sides of the podium. Without it, she just might collapse. She peeked over at Mike and appreciated his smile and nod.

"Mayor." She licked her lips and tried to swallow, but her mouth was too dry. Her sweat stole all the moisture. "Councilmen.

Uh. Wom—members."

Get a grip. Take a deep breath. Start again. Lord, help me.

"The, ah, um. . ."

Rats. Try again.

She glanced at her notes. Somehow she'd gotten them out of order. She lifted her gaze to the room full of people, all watching her intently. Swallowing hard, she opened her mouth. "Twenty percent of Americans have never used e-mail." Yes, that was what she'd meant to say. Good. "Most of that percentage can't afford Internet service. Of those who do have Internet, only half manage to come up with the money for high speed."

Where did that come from? Keep going.

She clutched the edges of her notes, her fingers icy cold. "Our library is behind—woefully behind—the times. We have one computer, which only has the capacity to help patrons locate books. I've checked other libraries in this county and in surrounding counties. They all have at least five computers, some boasting ten, all Internet capable. Our library is small and can't hold all the books citizens seek. Though we do have inter-library loan, there's still much more available on the Internet. If we want to provide the service our patrons deserve, we need to offer several computers so each citizen who can't afford Internet service can find the help they need in their local library."

Goodness. I'm out of breath. Talk about the money.

She eyed the council members the way she'd seen Ken do. "The way I have it figured, if we started with five computers and printers, all with high-speed Internet capability, we should be able to buy them and all the software for under eight thousand dollars. There's still the installation fees. I'll have to check into that and get back to you. But I can't imagine it'd take much over fifteen thousand. In fact, it might not even be that much."

"She's up to full steam, boys." Veronica's voice cut through her thoughts.

Of all the dirty, rotten. . . Monah knew Veronica was only here to cause trouble.

"Get your hose, Ken," Veronica continued. "She's talking so fast there's got to be smoke billowing. And we all know where there's smoke, there's fire."

Laughter rumbled through the room. Heat rose in Monah's face. Fighting anger, she gripped the edges of the podium.

Ken motioned as if he were hosing her down. "There. I think she's out."

The mayor cleared his throat in disapproval, but before he could intervene, Mike straightened. "No need for that, Ken."

While she appreciated Mike's protectiveness, Monah knew now was not the time to let him fight her battles. She turned to face Ken. "I didn't interrupt when you were speaking."

He crossed his arms. "Aw, come on, Monah. You can't really believe your computers are more important than upgrading our fire station. Next thing we know, you'll want to serve coffee with your computers."

Monah bristled. Now he sounded like Miss Tait. "Food and beverages aren't allowed in the library. We're there to feed brains, not bellies."

"Yeah, well, people can't learn if they're dead."

She was losing the battle. If Ken continued comparing computers to lives, she didn't stand a chance. "Which is exactly why I'm not asking for all of the money, Ken, only a portion, and a small portion at that. Lives are important, yes, but so is the education of our children and grandchildren." She cast a quick glance around the room. "Who in here wants to send their children off to college without the basic knowledge for conducting simple research? Isn't the job market competitive enough?"

Ken shook his head. "That's stretching it, don't you think?"

"Actually, no, I don't." She drew a deep breath to continue.

"Miss Trenary, your time has expired," Mayor Wright interrupted.

"B–but, but—," Monah stammered.

The mayor held up his hand. "I'm sorry, Monah, but fair's fair. Everyone is allowed the same amount of time."

Drat. Thanks to Veronica's interruption, she hadn't even mentioned a possible Web site, access to college applications, free online job postings, or the dozen other things she'd meant to touch on. Gathering her papers, she stepped away from the podium. "Okay, Mr. Mayor, but despite what Ken or anyone else might think," she cast a final glare in Veronica's direction, "educating and equipping our children is every bit as important as making sure they sleep safely at night." Drawing a deep breath, she faced the council members one last time. "Thank you for your time."

Chin raised high, Monah made her way down the stairs. She'd made her point, maybe not the way she'd wanted but well enough. Even Ken would have to admit her argument had weight. In fact, a few people near the rear of the room nodded their heads at her as if to say, "Good job." Pride swelled her chest. She drew her shoulders back and headed for the door. She'd done it after all. She'd shown that council—

Monah gave a yelp. Her toe caught in the handle of Mrs. Teaser's cat-shaped knitting bag. Unable to catch herself, she sprawled face first on the floor.

"My goodness, are you all right, dear?" Sympathy etched the elderly woman's face.

"I'm fine," Monah mumbled.

Her dramatic exit ruined, Monah jumped to her feet and scurried to the door, Veronica's laughter ringing behind her.

CHAPTER THIRTEEN

Mike shoved aside his cup, half filled with cold coffee, and slid back his chair. This was nuts. He hadn't been able to concentrate all morning. A steady drizzle that started before dawn still poured outside his window. It made his office gray and filled the station with a damp, musty odor. By the muffled laughter drifting down the hall, the other officers must be struggling to concentrate as well. He dropped his gaze to the folder spread on the desk in front of him. From an old photo, Charlotte Tait peered up at him through thick spectacles. Next to her lay a list of suspects he'd spent all morning compiling. A shaky list, he corrected, based on half a dozen conversations. Arguments, rumors, people in the library the day she died—it all amounted to a heaping plate of circumstantial nothing.

Heaving a sigh, he scanned the names, most of which he'd already committed to memory. When he reached Monah's, he ran his index finger over the letters. No way he'd ever believe her capable of murder. It wasn't in her makeup, not for any amount of money. The memory of her troubled face at the city council meeting the other night sure bothered him though. She could be single-minded when she wanted to be, dogged even. He shook his head. No. Not Monah.

So who did that leave? He continued down the list. Jamie

Canon, Ken Greer, Robin Beck—

"Detective Brockman?"

Mike started then rubbed a hand over his face. He'd have to warn Parker about sneaking up on him. "Come on in."

Parker eased toward the desk, a folder in his hand. "I was filing and found this mixed in with last year's stuff. Figured you'd want to see it."

Mike immediately recognized the lettering. The arson cases. How'd that get mixed up with the others? He scooted out his chair and took the file. "Glad you spotted this. I'll take care of it."

Parker moved to leave but hesitated at the door. "Funny how all this trouble started around the same time, eh?"

Pausing at the filing cabinet, Mike rested his palm on the handle. "What?"

"You know. . .the fires, Miss Tait, the bickering over the money—it all started around the same time."

It sure did. As Parker left, Mike ran the back of his fingers over his stubbly cheek, considering that, then walked to his desk and picked up both folders. His gaze shifted from one to the other. Parker was right. The trouble did all start around the same time. Could it be all three were connected? What if the person who killed Miss Tait had a vested interest in not only the money but the fires as well?

Encouraged for the first time that morning, he flipped open the arsons folder. So far the damaged properties had one thing in common—they were deserted or vacant. But who owned them? He pulled up the tax office on the Internet and typed in the first 911 address. Wayne Drolen? Mike's fingers hovered over the keyboard as a spark of excitement ignited in his belly. Wayne certainly had an interest in the funds donated to the city. He'd put a dent in his own pocketbook securing a publicist for his sports complex—a fact that put him squarely at odds with Charlotte Tait. That gave him motive for murder, and the fires could be tied to insurance money.

Fingers flying, he typed the next address. No luck. Greg Dyer owned the abandoned warehouse that went up last week. He moved down the list. Of the seven properties, Wayne Drolen owned three—a boathouse and two abandoned houses. Not conclusive but intriguing, especially since Wayne could easily have ordered the additional fires to divert attention.

He picked up the list of suspects. This time he focused on a single person—city councilman Wayne Drolen.

~

"Here's the last of it."

Monah tugged a box from the bed of her father's truck and set it on the table already stacked with books. "I sure hope they all sell at this fund-raiser. After the disaster at the council meeting, I'll need every penny they bring in. I doubt anyone would vote to give me a dime of that donated money after I made such a fool of myself."

Casey emptied the box and arranged the books by genre. "I can't believe it was as bad as you say."

"Yeah, well, if you'd been there, you'd know it was probably worse." A shudder coursed through her as the night replayed in her mind.

"I told you, Aunt Liddy didn't feel well. I thought I should stay with her, but I really am sorry I didn't at least phone."

Monah dropped into one of the two lawn chairs she'd brought. "I understand. I would've done the same. But I sure needed some support that night."

Casey's face fell into a sympathetic frown. "I know. I'm sorry. When will they decide on the money?"

"I'm not sure. I didn't stick around to find out. I can ask Mike when he gets here."

Casey froze, staring at a book in her hands, then turned the cover toward Monah. "You're selling the Brandy Purcell books? Why would you get rid of them? They're everyone's favorites."

With a smile, Monah started to relax. She wanted to enjoy the day. "They're extras. I didn't think the library needed three copies."

"Oh. In that case, I'll let them go." Casey plopped into the chair next to her. "Putting up your parents' canopy was a good idea. Looks like we're in for a scorcher today." She propped her feet on one of the two large coolers. "And bringing these bottles of water to give away was a stroke of genius. They ought to fetch people here in droves."

"That was the plan. Come by for water and browse in the shade."

Monah turned her attention to Ken and his volunteer fire-fighters as they prepped their biggest and newest fire truck for visitors. Several pairs of boots lined the sidewalk, all waiting to accept donations. The men would parade the streets seeking any and all loose change from willing contributors. Ken had even managed to convince the hospital manager to park an ambulance next to the fire truck. Those interested could peek inside. Oh, but was he ever a smooth talker.

No sooner had she formed the thought than Ken turned and gave her his usual two-finger salute. She pinched her lips together.

"Don't let him get to you."

Monah turned toward Casey. "Easier said than done. He's right next to us."

"I know, but just ignore him so we can have some fun."

"I'm all for that."

She adjusted her chair to face the opposite direction. Across and down the street, some of Mike's officers had set up a dunking booth. He'd told her it was just for fun. They'd give away candy and stickers that looked like badges to the children. The adults would get the satisfaction of seeing Pine Mills's finest all wet. Monah smiled. Mike would take a turn on the seat. She might have to see how accurate her arm was when his time rolled around.

Several other vendors looking to make a little money were putting up their own booths. She waved at Mary Bowen busily displaying her homemade goodies, then at Willa Teale, the local antique dealer. Earl Trigg set out his wood carvings while his wife, Margaret, strategically hung her handmade jewelry around and on the wood art. What had started as a small fund-raising idea had turned into a street fair. Ken even promised fireworks at the end of the day. Yep, he was a smooth one. Knew how to play the people.

Casey bumped Monah's elbow. "Look." She pointed down the blocked-off street. "It's not even ten o'clock, and they're starting to flock."

Monah grinned. "You know what they say about the early bird." She leaned forward and grabbed a bottle of water from the cooler. "And my bookworms are more than ready."

Interest in the offered books was more than Monah had anticipated. In just over an hour, most of the children's books were gone, thrilling her to no end. She'd started to believe people had lost interest in reading, but they'd proved her wrong. She grabbed her cell phone and punched in Sandy's number.

"Sandy," she hollered into the phone when her co-worker answered, "remember that 'just in case' box I left on the chair in the library office? Would you mind swinging by there and getting it for me? I'm almost out of kids' books."

At Sandy's affirmative, Monah slapped the phone closed and grinned at Casey. "I'm so excited to see that children still like to read. I thought it might be going the way of the horse and carriage."

"Ain't it the truth?" Dena Drolen stood next to the table and rapped her knuckles on one of the books. "I've been so afraid that kids nowadays are too wrapped up in television, the Internet, or those silly headset things hooked in their ears to care much about reading. I'm glad to learn that I'm wrong."

Monah pulled her into a hug. "A woman after my own heart." She leaned back. "I haven't seen you lately. You must have straightened out the post office."

"I think so. They guaranteed me I was getting everything." She narrowed her eyes. "Why? Do you have some of my mail?"

Laughter bubbled in Monah's chest. "Not that I'm aware of. I guess our bellyaching did the trick."

"It's about time." Dena mopped at the perspiration dripping from her forehead and cheeks. "Goodness, it's a hot one today."

Monah opened a cooler and grabbed a bottle. "I'm sorry, Dena. I should have offered you some water. Get me started talking about books, and you can see what happens."

Dena held the bottle out and tilted her head up in order to use her bifocals to read what Monah printed on each bottle. " 'Love your local library.' Well, isn't that cute. It could be taken two ways. You're so creative, Monah." She pressed the cold container against her neck and closed her eyes. "That feels heavenly."

"I'll bet." She smiled at Dena's obvious pleasure. "I'd heard it was supposed to be hot today, and I figured if everyone knew they'd get free water it would draw them over to look at the books."

"Absolutely brilliant." She opened the bottle and took a long drink. "I don't suppose you'd let me have another one for Wayne."

Ugh. He should at least come and ask for one himself. "Sure. No problem." She flipped open the lid, saw the bottles were gone, and grabbed one from the second cooler. "Here you go."

"Thank you, dear. I'll be sure to let him know it's from his favorite local library."

With a wink and a wave, Dena faded into the crowd. Her hands on her hips, Monah wondered why Wayne couldn't be as sweet as his wife. Not wanting to waste time thinking about that man, she busied herself placing more bottled water in the empty cooler. Now, where did Casey disappear to? Monah spotted her raving to a woman about the Brandy Purcell books, almost shoving them into the poor lady's hands.

The ear-piercing squeal of kids grabbed her attention. Ken was spraying water from a large hose into the air. The children laughed as they danced in the sprinkles. Just as the thought entered her mind that he'd better not point the water her way, spatters hit the canopy. She raced through the shower.

"Ken!" She ran faster, getting soaked. "Don't you dare get my books wet. Point that hose the other way." When she reached him, she shook her finger under his nose. "You've got the whole yard behind you to aim the water. Now move that hose before you ruin my books."

With a grin and his two-fingered salute, he changed directions. Monah caught his wink at one of his workers, and she wanted to smack him. Instead, she stomped back to her booth, her good mood gone.

Casey dabbed up the drops that had managed to hit the table and books along the edge. "You know he did that on purpose."

"I know it. I don't understand why he thought it necessary.

He did a much better job speaking to the council than I did." She glared at him. "Guess he felt the need to make a joke of me one more time."

"There's no real damage done." Casey tossed the towel onto a lawn chair. "Let it go, or he'll have accomplished what he set out to do."

"What? Ruin my day?"

"Yep."

They both did another quick check of the tables to make sure they didn't miss any wet spots.

"Did it rain when I wasn't looking?" Mike put his arms around Monah from behind and gave her a quick hug. "There's not a cloud in the sky."

She spun in his arms and returned the gesture. "Don't get me started. I'd rather forget about Ken and his antics and dig into lunch."

She set one of the extra lawn chairs next to hers and the other beside Casey's. Luke sauntered up and pulled Casey into his arms. Monah gestured to them. "Break it up, you two. I'm starved. Let's eat."

The look on Mike's face stopped her cold. She'd seen it too many times. He was standing her up. "What?"

"I tried to call you."

"When?"

"About three times in the last half hour."

She believed him but still needed to check. She snatched up her cell phone. Three missed calls. "What happened? We were supposed to have a picnic together. You're the one who asked me." This was definitely not her day.

"I know." He pulled her back into his arms. "I'm sorry, but the mayor wants me to share a lunch with him. There's something he wants to discuss."

"About the donated funds?"

Mike grinned. "I doubt it."

"Well, if so, be sure to put in a good word for me."

He gave her a quick peck on the lips. "You got it. I'll come by when we're through."

"You'd better."

When she could no longer see him, she flopped onto her chair. "This day couldn't get any worse."

Luke sat next to her and handed her a sandwich from the picnic basket he brought. "Don't say that, or it just might."

Reluctantly, Monah agreed. She nibbled on her sandwich, then got up to rearrange the book tables.

Two hours passed. Monah scanned the busy street for Mike's tall form among the milling throng. Colorful balloons bobbed on the summer breeze, and though plenty of people lined up in front of the dunking booth, there was still no sign of Mike. What in the world did the mayor have to say for so long? The only bright spot was the fact that many of the books were gone. Keeping a running tally in her head, Monah figured the library had made close to three hundred dollars.

Commotion from the other side of the dunking booth pulled her from her musings. This wasn't the happy laughter she'd heard earlier. This sounded more like panic. She ran over and elbowed her way through.

On her knees, Dena Drolen leaned over Wayne, who lay crumpled on the ground, his face pasty white, a sheen of perspiration dotting his forehead and lip.

An emergency vehicle wove through the barriers erected on the end of the street and screamed to a stop next to them. The paramedic who drove the ambulance shoved Dena out of the way and knelt beside Wayne. After checking his pulse, the medic cleaned out Wayne's mouth, inserted a small plastic device to blow into, and adjusted his head. Then he puffed into Wayne's mouth and pumped on his chest while a second paramedic yanked equipment out of the ambulance.

"Anyone who knows CPR, give me a hand," the medic huffed between each pump. "I need someone to blow in his mouth."

Stuck in a fog of shock, Monah didn't move. She knew a little CPR. She'd taken classes several years ago.

Get down there and help.

"Someone, help me!"

A jostle to her side woke her from her daze. Mike dropped to his knees and blew into Wayne's mouth as the paramedic counted out the chest compressions. Relief and pride washed through her that Mike had stepped up.

"I'm ready," the man with the equipment said.

The first paramedic shoved Mike's hands away and ripped open Wayne's shirt. "Stay clear. We're gonna shock him."

The defibrillator whined and then jolted Wayne. Almost immediately, the two men resumed working on him. Sweat rolled down their faces and dripped from their chins. They both panted from the exertion. Then Ted Levy tapped the paramedic on the shoulder.

"Let me spell you here. You take Mike's place."

Without breaking the rhythm, the medical examiner took over the compressions while Mike moved out of the paramedic's way. Another shock and labor that spanned several minutes followed before Ted stopped to check the pulse and listen to the heart one more time. He shook his head and sat back.

"He's gone. We can't help him."

"Noooooo!"

Dena dropped on top of her lifeless husband. Sobs racked her as she shook his body. She peppered his face with kisses, her tears leaving wet spots on his skin. Holding his face between her hands, she pleaded for him to come back.

Her throat tight with emotion, Monah scooted next to Dena and put her arm around her shaking shoulders. Dena looked up and then pressed her face against Monah's neck, her wails reaching a crescendo. Monah's tears mixed with Dena's as the howls turned to quiet, heartrending moans.

Mike touched her shoulder. "Let's get her out of here."

He helped Monah and Dena to their feet and stepped back to allow the paramedic closer with his gurney. Just as he and a couple of men lifted Wayne's body, the fire truck's siren wailed. Several volunteer firemen jumped on the truck as Ken blew the horn and headed down the street. In the distance, huge billows of black smoke filled the air.

CHAPTER FOURTEEN

Disbelief warred with compassion inside Mike's head as he stared at Wayne Drolen's lifeless body. A second later, the closing of the ambulance doors hid it from view. Mike had been so sure he was on to something back at the station. Could he have been wrong?

Dena's quiet sobbing added an odd counterpoint to the lively music drifting from one of the concession stands. Mike flashed a grimace at the owner, who promptly shut it off, freeing him to think clearly.

When Mike had arrived, Wayne Drolen's face was chalky white. A thin sheen of perspiration made his skin appear glossy. Both were symptoms from another case. He whirled toward Dena. "Mrs. Drolen, I'm so very sorry for your loss. I know this is a bad time, but I've got a few questions for you." He gestured toward the shade of a spreading oak. "It'll only take a moment."

"Mike!" Monah hissed.

Dena shook her head and pulled out of Monah's grasp to stumble toward the ambulance. "The hospital. . .I've got to get to the hospital with Wayne."

"They're not taking him to the hospital," he said softly.

She peered up at him, her eyes welling with fresh tears. "W—what?"

Mike stepped toward her, his foot connecting with a half-empty water bottle. He bent to pick it up.

"I'll take that. It's Wayne's. He dropped it when—" She groaned and covered her face with both hands. Muttering words of sympathy, Monah slipped her arm around Dena's shoulders and pulled her close.

Mike looked at the label on the water bottle in his hand, his memory sparking back to Charlotte's death. He lifted his head. "Mrs. Drolen, who gave you this water?"

"I did." Monah frowned. "Why?"

He flashed a quick glance at her, and to his own dismay, he felt his official facade slide into place. "Just curious." He turned to Dena. "Was Wayne sick before coming to the fund-raiser today?"

She shook her head. "No, though he did complain of his stomach being upset just before. . .before. . ."

"That's okay. I understand." Mike took out his handkerchief and wrapped it carefully around the bottle. "Did he throw up that you can remember?"

She shuddered. "I'm not sure. He went to the bathroom," she ended on a whisper.

"Was anyone else around?"

"No. We were walking back when he collapsed."

Monah's eyes narrowed. "Where are you going with this, Mike?"

Suddenly, the ambulance engine revved, and the vehicle prepared to carry its cargo to the county morgue. A tiny sound escaped Dena, and she swung her head to search the row of cars. "They're leaving. I've got to go."

The rest of Mike's questions would have to wait. He wouldn't keep a grieving widow from spending these last few precious moments saying good-bye to her husband. "No problem, Mrs.

Drolen. Can I get you a ride?"

"I'll take care of it." Monah cast a reassuring smile at Dena. "Don't worry about a thing."

Dena nodded, her face as lost and pathetic as a child's. A small number of the crowd began sidling away, tossing a last few, occasional glances in their direction. Officials dispersed the rest as the ambulance picked its way up the street.

Before Monah could pull Dena away, Mike bent close to her ear. "Will you stay with her until family arrives?" She nodded, and he moved to Ted. Taking his arm, he led him away from listening ears. "Find out what happened. I wanna know what killed this man. Now. Whatever you have to do. . ."

Ted nodded, his gaze somber. Tugging his keys from his pocket, Mike jogged down the street to his car. After slipping Wayne's half-empty water bottle into a plastic bag and stowing it in the glove compartment, he slammed the door and started the engine. There was nothing more to do here, and Ken and the other volunteer firemen could use his help. The scanner chirped the conversation between Ken and the station, so though Mike knew where the fire was located, the smoke would have been easy enough to follow, regardless. Within minutes, he pulled to a stop behind the Pine Mills Fire Department trucks, near an open field.

Flames licked greedily at the trees and parched grass. Hissing like an angry cat, the fire was an intimidating sight as it raced over the field. At the rate the fire consumed ground, it wouldn't be long before the farmhouse perched a few hundred yards on the horizon was in danger. Shedding his gun and badge, Mike jumped from his car and raced to take a spot on the fire hose. The heat as he drew nearer blistered his skin, and the smell of wood smoke combined with floating ash made his eyes water.

Stepping forward, Ken shoved firmly on Mike's chest. "No

way," he shouted above the screaming of the fire engines and hiss of the fire. He grabbed the collar of his flame-retardant coat. "Not without one of these."

Mike pointed at the farmhouse. "Wanna explain that to them?"

Ken's gaze followed where he pointed. "Okay," he said with a reluctant nod. "But you stay behind Joe, here." He clapped the shoulder of a volunteer fireman struggling with the bulging water hose then looked back at Mike. "Make sure you keep the spray in front of you. It'll beat down the heat. Joe, keep an eye on the probie."

His face already blackened by soot, Joe flashed a toothy grin at Mike before turning back to the flames. "You got it, Chief."

But Ken was already gone, racing around the edge of the field toward a row of firefighters frantically digging a trench to stop the progression of the fire.

"Let's go, probie!" Joe shouted. He pointed toward the men at the trench. "We gotta give them some relief."

Wrestling the hose to their shoulders, Mike and two other volunteers followed Joe across the scorched field. At first, their progress appeared slow, but then the fire department from a neighboring county arrived. Together the two crews brought the blaze under control.

Only when most of the smoke had cleared and the flames were reduced to smoldering ash did Mike relinquish his spot on the hose.

Joe flashed him a cocky grin. "Good job, probie. We'll make a fireman outta ya yet."

Mike coughed to clear the burning in his throat and returned the grin. "I meant to ask—probie?"

"Probationary. Speaking of which," Joe tossed the now-lax hose toward Mike, "it's the probie's job to wind the hose. Have fun."

A shout of laughter went up from the firefighters gathered around. A couple of them leaned wearily against the side of the fire truck. Mike shook his head and reached for the hose. They were a good group of guys. They worked hard and earned nothing, but they were always ready to laugh.

"They're breaking you in good, I see."

Ken sauntered across the blackened grass, a wide grin splitting his lips. Like the other firefighters, he was covered in dirt and soot, and sweat carved greasy trails down his face. Mike looked exactly the same. He finished winding the hose onto the fire truck then wiped his hands on his pant legs.

"Never say I didn't bother getting to know how you make a living."

Ken chuckled and handed him a bottled water. "You got it."

After unscrewing the cap, Mike tipped up the bottle and took a long swig. "Ah," he said, drawing his hand across his mouth, "water never tasted so good."

"You'll want to drink plenty when you get home. It'll hit you later otherwise."

Mike nodded and started toward his car, Ken close behind. "Well?"

He didn't need to elaborate. Ken knew exactly what he was asking. He shrugged. "Could've been anything, a cigarette butt even. This type of fire is harder to unravel."

Mike figured as much. He looked around at the extensive charring that stretched clear across the field and into the tree line. "Any idea who owns this land?"

Ken rubbed his chin. "Not really. I could find out though."

"Do that." Mike opened his car door and threw the empty water bottle inside.

"Got something in mind?"

"Maybe." He rested his arm on the roof, fingers drumming the hot metal. "At least I thought so, before Drolen keeled over."

"About that. . ." Ken's brow furrowed in a frown. "Any idea what happened?"

"Not yet. Ted's working on it. I should hear something soon."

Ken shook his head. "I don't get it. The guy was fairly young and in good shape. What makes a man like him suddenly drop dead?"

Mike had been wondering the same thing. He wasn't jumping to conclusions, but his gut told him Ted's report would rule out natural causes.

Ken eyed him steadily. Mike straightened and closed the door. He and Ken had been buddies a long time, and though he enjoyed working with him and his crew, he wasn't free to share his hunches just yet. "Guess I'd better get back, see what I can do to help Dena."

"The guys and I will get together, maybe take up a collection for flowers or something."

Mike nodded and circled to the driver's side. "If you do happen to find out anything—"

"I'll let you know."

He rapped on the roof as Mike climbed in and slammed the door. "Be careful. Drink water!"

His shout penetrated the confines of the car as Mike started the engine and rumbled onto the road. Ken was a good guy. A little too enthusiastic, maybe, and gung ho on his job but then, so was Mike.

Catching a glimpse of his grimy reflection in the rearview mirror, Mike sighed. Better swing by home first so he could shower and change before heading to the Drolens'. Mentally, he began preparing a list of questions: Had Wayne been known to have health issues? Was there a history of heart problems in his family? This was not a task he relished, but it was necessary. And at some point, he wanted—no, needed—to call Monah.

Thinking of her stirred tension in his gut. Two people, both known adversaries for the city's donated funds, had dropped dead from suspicious causes in her presence. He clenched the steering wheel and shook the notion loose. Twenty other residents of Pine Mills had also been present. He had no reason to be particularly interested in Monah, not as a cop anyway.

That still did not explain the water bottles. *Easy*, he told himself. Anybody could have slipped something into the water when Monah wasn't looking. A sliver of guilt wriggled through his conscience. Maybe his growing feelings for her obstructed his judgment. Maybe he couldn't see clearly where she was concerned. Absently, he turned off the highway onto the road leading home. If he were honest, he'd have to admit he was far more inclined to believe the best of her than anyone else. But hadn't his years in police work taught him to consider everyone? Hadn't he learned that even the people most innocent in appearance often turned out to be guilty?

He slapped the steering wheel in a sudden flash of anger. *No!* Monah wasn't capable of evil. He wouldn't allow himself to become so jaded that he stooped to suspecting everyone, even the love of his life.

Instinctively, his foot pressed the accelerator at the unexpected revelation. Hearing the engine growl, he checked the speedometer and forced himself to slow down.

So there it was—the truth. He loved her. What normally should have filled him with joy brought no pleasure. Despite his feelings, he had a job to do, and he couldn't allow anyone, not even Monah, to stand in his way.

CHAPTER FIFTEEN

"Are you sure you don't want me to come along, Dena?"
Monah held the car door open while the sorrow-filled woman dropped into the front seat. "I really don't mind. I think you need to be with someone right now, and I'm not sure it's a good idea for you to be driving."

Dena grabbed Monah's free hand and squeezed. "You've been such a help, dear, but it's totally unnecessary for you to accompany me. Besides, I need some time alone to think. And cry." More tears pursued the previous ones. She shook her head. "I can't believe this is happening."

"That's why I should go with you. Plus, I promised Mike I would stay until your family arrives. If nothing else, I can at least hold you while we cry together."

Monah meant every word. She and Wayne may not have been friends, but that didn't stop her from sympathizing with Dena at such an awful time.

Dena rose from the car seat and pulled Monah into a quick hug. "I appreciate everything you've tried to do, really. But there will be plenty of people around me in the days ahead. . .and right now"—she choked on a sob and twisted her wedding band around on her finger—"I have to be alone, even if just for a few minutes." Drawing a breath to compose herself, she wiped away her tears then patted Monah's arm. "I promise, if I need anything, I'll call you."

Catching Dena's hand in a last-ditch effort of persuasion, Monah gave her fingers a squeeze. "At least let me find you a ride. Mike would be worried sick if he knew you were driving in this condition."

Dena's head had already begun to shake. She sat again and grasped the door handle. "I'm a politician's wife. Believe me, I know how to handle stress, but I need these few moments of privacy to get ready for what lies ahead. Now, I've gotta go. I don't want to get too far behind Wayne."

Before Monah could say a word, Dena yanked the door closed, started the car, and raced out of the parking lot. Monah waited until she could no longer see the car then, heaving a sigh, went to help Casey finish boxing up the rest of the books, her mind roiling with thoughts of Wayne's death. None of it made a bit of sense.

"He was too young."

Casey stopped taping flaps closed and looked at her. "Who? Wayne?"

"Yeah." Monah rested her arms on the edges of a box. "What was he, about fifty? That's too young to just drop dead."

She hefted her box and walked toward her dad's truck with Casey doing the same. The memory of Wayne lying on the ground ran through her head as she dropped the tailgate and shoved the box inside. After Casey placed hers next to the other, Monah leaned against the fender.

"Did any of that seem familiar to you?" She paused and stared into Casey's eyes. "Think about it. The pale face and sweaty skin. . ." A shudder shook her.

"You're talking about Miss Tait."

"Exactly."

"You think Wayne was murdered, too?"

Monah shrugged. "It sure seems like an odd coincidence. But why?"

"Who knows? Why would anyone want to kill Miss Tait?" Casey propped her hip against the tailgate. "None of it makes sense, but you sure have piqued my curiosity to the point where I won't sleep tonight for thinking about it."

A burst of energy pulsed through Monah and pushed aside the weariness she fought. She grabbed Casey's elbow. "Me either. So how about we head over to the library or stop for a bite to eat and try to decipher all of this? Let's figure out if any of the people around Wayne were the same ones at the library the day Miss Tait died."

"You've got to be kidding." Casey's statement could have been discouraging except for the grin on her face. "Don't you remember how many people were milling around? Every citizen of Pine Mills made an appearance on this very street."

"Okay, so it won't be easy, but I'm game for a late night of sleuthing. How about you?"

Casey patted the purse hanging over her shoulder. "My Post-its are in here, so I'm all set. Besides, I doubt Ken will still set off the fireworks display after fighting a fire."

"Yeah, how weird was that, having both things happen at the same time? If we get a chance, I'd really like to look into those arsons a bit and see if we can come up with something Mike has overlooked." She headed back to the tables to take them down along with the canopy. "I hope he checks in to let me know he's all right."

"He will." Casey fell into step alongside her. "When he calls, we can mention the similarities in the deaths."

Remembering the look on Mike's face, Monah shrugged. She picked up the first table and folded the legs. "Actually, I think he's already put those two together. Did you see how he slipped into cop mode when he questioned Dena?"

"It's his job, Monah."

"I know, but maybe we can put our heads together with him and find out who's eliminating our residents."

"And make sure he knows you could be next."

The table fell from Monah's fingers with a thud. "What?"

"You want the donated funds as bad as Miss Tait and Wayne did. That could be the connection."

Monah swallowed hard. "Or the motive."

~

The clink of ice hitting glass was the only sound in Mike's otherwise too-quiet kitchen. He'd showered, and remembering his promise to Ken to drink plenty of water, he had pulled a bottle from his refrigerator to pour over the cubes.

Bottled water.

Mike grimaced. Looked innocent enough. Could someone have used it as a murder weapon? He'd have to get Wayne's bottle out of the glove compartment and deliver it to Ted as soon as he left Dena's place. Which reminded him. . .

The clock on the microwave said 5:37. It was getting late. He'd have to hurry.

He filled his glass then downed the icy liquid. Snatching his keys off the countertop, he strode from the kitchen to the front door of his tiny apartment. Tony and Raoul, the kids from next door, yelled his name as he stepped outside.

"Officer Mike!" The younger of the two, Raoul, shook his baseball mitt off his hand and rushed across the lawn. The older brother, Tony, followed.

"It's *Detective*, stupid," Tony said, elbowing his younger brother in the ribs. His disgusted gaze swung off his brother and brightened when it met Mike's. "He never gets it right."

Raoul's face fell. "I forgot again."

Mike grinned and ruffled the boy's ebony hair. "No problem, kiddo. You guys staying out of trouble?"

"Yes, sir," they chimed in unison.

Raoul's round brown eyes glinted with laughter. "Mama said we're supposed to listen to everything you say. She likes you."

"Stupid," Tony hissed again.

Mike dropped to squat in front of Raoul. "How's she doing? Things better now that she's working?"

Giving a serious nod, Raoul's dark head bobbed. "She really likes the nursing home. Sometimes she lets us go with her if she's not too busy."

"That's good."

Mike stood and placed his hand on Tony's thin shoulder. Older than his brother by almost four years, Tony took it upon himself to look out for Raoul, especially since their father, a soldier, returned home in a casket almost a year ago. The boys' mother did what she could, but raising two rambunctious kids on her own, plus working full-time, left little time for anything else. "Take it easy on your brother, eh, Tony?"

Tony smiled and gave a meek shrug. "Okay, Detective Mike."

Mike pulled his keys from his pocket. "I'll see you later, boys. Be good now."

One of Tony's raven eyebrows quirked. "You going to that lady's house?"

"The lady?" Mike paused. "You mean Mrs. Drolen? How did you know about that?"

"Everybody knows."

"I even know," Raoul piped up, skipping away several steps then skipping back. "I saw the dead guy. Tony saw him, too. He was all white and stuff."

Mike's protective instincts went into overdrive. No kid should have to witness a death. "I'm sorry you saw that."

"I'm not. It was cool! I'm gonna be a doctor."

The randomness of his thoughts settled the worry clutching Mike's gut. Raoul would be fine.

"Maybe it was the lady," Raoul continued. "Maybe she punched him 'cuz she was mad. They were fighting."

"Not fighting, stupid, arguing." Tony smacked his brother on the arm, and then he looked apologetically at Mike. "Raoul had to go to the bathroom. We'd just left when Mr. and Mrs. Drolen walked up. He looked really sick, but Mrs. Drolen yelled at him anyway. Guess that's why they didn't see us."

Mike bent over, his hands on his knees, to look directly into Tony's eyes. "Could you hear what they were saying?"

"Mrs. Drolen kept saying he wasn't paying enough attention to her."

"And she was worried about the money," Raoul said, bouncing on his toes eagerly.

"Money?" Mike turned his head to the younger boy.

"Yeah. Money, money, money." He spoke the words in a singsong voice, his head tilting each time. "'Gotta take care of the money. Gotta have the money.' She sounded like Mama before—"

"Before you helped her find a job," Tony said, not about to be outdone by his baby brother.

Mike straightened. So, maybe the rumors were true. Wayne Drolen had hired a publicist with money out of his own pocket. Could that have been what he and Dena were arguing about moments before he died?

"Thanks, guys. You two stay out of trouble now."

"Yes, sir," they said, then scampered away to finish their game of catch.

With even more to think about, Mike barely noticed the drive across town to the Drolen residence. Pulling up to the stately home did, however, remind him of something Ted had said earlier: *"He's way too worried about his reputation on the city council."*

Yes, this house screamed reputation. Tall pillars stood sentry before a massive oak door fitted with leaded glass. Mike walked past three expensive cars parked in front of the house and mounted the curving steps. A porcelain doorbell rested inside an intricately carved case. Mike pushed it and waited. From within, a soft melody chimed. Seconds later, the door swung open. An austere woman dressed in black eyed him critically.

"Yes?"

Mike pulled his badge from his jacket pocket. "Detective Mike Brockman here to see Dena Drolen."

The woman stepped back a pace. "This way."

Her soft-soled shoes made little noise as she led him down the hall to a large study. Wayne's study, by the masculine look of the room. A framed degree from the University of Massachusetts hung on the wall behind the desk. Next to a tortoiseshell pencil cup sat a glossy black humidor. Funny, Mike didn't know Drolen smoked. As silently as she'd appeared, the woman in black eased from the study and closed the door behind her.

"Detective?"

Mike turned, totally unprepared for the sight that met his eyes.

CHAPTER ⫟⫟⫟ SIXTEEN

The air inside the library was cool and dry, much better than the temperature outside. Monah dropped a box of books on the counter and turned to Casey. "So, where's the best place to start our research? The people wanting the funds? Or the arsons, like who owned the properties? Oh, wait. We can list who owned the properties and see which ones match those fighting for the money."

Casey laughed. "I think we should start by booting up the computer."

Monah made a face. "Oh, right. Sometimes I get carried away."

"Ya think?" Casey sat at the counter and pulled the Post-its from her purse. "While you do that, I'll start writing down the locations of the fires."

Half an hour later, Monah sat back in her chair. "Unbelievable. Wayne Drolen owned three of the burned properties."

"Yeah, except now he's dead." Casey raised her brows. "What do you make of that?"

Monah bumped her glasses back in place. "I have no idea." Seconds later, she sat up straight. "Wait. You don't think he's dead *because* of the fires, do you?"

Casey frowned. "I don't follow. What do you mean?"

"What if someone was after Wayne, like burning his property before going after him?" She shrugged. "Probably a long shot."

"Maybe. Maybe not." Casey leaned toward the keyboard and hit a key that pulled up the list of Wayne's properties. "Then again, it's possible he burned them down himself to get the insurance money. He could have used that money to pay that publicity woman you told me about. But would he be that bold. . .or dumb?"

"Or desperate?" Monah rubbed her chin. "Do you think they all burned down completely?"

"I don't know. Why?"

Excitement grew as an idea formed. "Let's go out and look around."

"What? Why?"

"We might find something."

Casey shook her head even as she smiled. "You don't think the police and Ken have been all through those places and found all there is to find?"

"Maybe. Maybe not." Monah grinned as she mimicked her friend's earlier comment. "It'll still be fun to explore." She rose. "Come on. It sure couldn't hurt."

"Isn't that trespassing? We could get into trouble."

"It's okay. I know the detective." Monah winked and laughed. "We'll start with the first one on the list and work our way down." She pulled up the entire list in alphabetical order and read. "Bingham's warehouse. Hey, wait." She leaned toward the computer screen. "Look." She pointed. "It was for sale, and Greg Dyer is the real estate agent. If we get caught, we can say we're potential customers."

Casey stood and grabbed her purse and the Post-it notes. "Right. I'm sure they'll buy that, especially since the place recently burned down."

"Yeah, but the land is still worth something, even if the warehouse is gone." Monah grabbed her hand and pulled her toward the door. "Oh, hush. I can tell by the look on your face you're just as excited to do this as I am."

"All right, but if we get arrested—"

"Won't happen. Trust me."

"Yeah, right."

They were pulling up to the burned-out warehouse when nerves took over and Monah had second thoughts. "You know, maybe—"

"Oh no, you don't. You got me here. We're going in." Casey already had her seat belt unbuckled and had pushed open the truck door. "Let's go, Sherlock."

Heart thumping as the excitement returned, Monah followed her friend to the entrance of the warehouse. It was unlocked.

Casey peeked inside then backed out. "I don't suppose your dad keeps a flashlight in his truck."

"Yeah, I think he does. Hang on." Rummaging under the seat, she pulled out two lights. She handed the larger one to Casey. "Ask and you shall receive."

The scent of smoke still hung heavy in the air. They'd surely smell like charcoal briquettes when they left. Their footsteps crunched in the rubble covering the flooring. The flashlight beam cut through the darkened interior like lightning across a stormy sky.

Monah aimed her light along the length of the building. "This place is huge." Her voice echoed. "Let's split up so we can cover more area. Shout if you find something."

Casey's brows winged upward, and she grabbed Monah's arm. "You know that's when people get killed, right? When they split up? I'm going with you."

Monah didn't want to admit it, but she was glad. There was something spooky about the place. "All right."

Her flashlight pointed at the floor, she started toward the back. She hoped and prayed she wouldn't see any mice or snakes. The thought sent a shudder through her, raising gooseflesh on her arms.

They made it all the way to the rear of the building without seeing anything of interest. Disappointment filled her, but she didn't want to give up. . .yet.

"Hey, I found something."

Casey's voice made Monah jump.

"What is it?"

"A door."

Monah moved to Casey's side. "The office, you think?"

"Those are usually near the front."

"A storage room?"

Casey pointed her beam right in Monah's eyes. "Isn't a warehouse one large storage room? And why are you whispering?"

Monah shoved the flashlight away from her face. "All right, smarty pants," she said in a louder voice that bounced back to her, making her cringe. "How about we just go in and find out what it is?"

"Sure. You first."

Go first? Monah swallowed the rush of saliva in her mouth. "Yeah. Uh, no problem."

She reached for the knob and turned. Unlocked. Hopefully, that was good news. She shuffled through the door. Casey nearly stepped on the heels of her shoes—she was so close. Monah swung her head to look at her. "Hey, stop pushing."

"Sorry."

A quick sweep of her light showed nothing but the remains of a table and a portable cart. "Rats."

"Where?" Casey grabbed Monah's arm and clutched it tight with one hand. With her other hand, she flicked her beam in a crazy dance all over the floor.

The hilarity of it all bubbled up until Monah couldn't help but giggle. "I didn't mean the critters. I meant it's a bummer there's nothing in here."

"Oh." Casey slapped her arm. "Well, don't use that word again. . .unless you mean those ugly varmints with beady eyes and whiskers. Then I want to know so I can run for the truck." She swung her light around the room again. "Can we go now?"

"Wait. We're here, and I'm sure I won't get you back again. Let's just take a closer look."

"Right. I'll stand here and provide the light."

This time Monah pointed her beam in Casey's eyes. "Chicken."

Monah moved to the table and looked around. Nothing. Around the cart, ashes formed soft mounds. She trained her light along the walls. A small piece of white caught her attention. She picked it up and held it to the light.

"What'd you find?" Casey still stood by the door.

"A piece of paper. It has some kind of printed words on it."

"What's it say?"

"I don't know. Most of it's burned off."

Casey finally entered the room and helped search for more paper. "Hey, here's one." She picked it up and kept looking. "And another. Both are burned, but the printing looks the same. Maybe if we try putting them together, we can come up with something complete."

Monah met her at the cart. They laid out the pieces they'd found. "What's that say—A-T-L?"

"This one has P-E-R."

"Atlper? Makes no sense. Let's look around and see if we can find any more."

They found nothing despite a thorough search. Everything else must have been destroyed by the fire. Disheartened, Monah leaned against the cart. It moved. She shoved it further, revealing more pieces of charred paper. Retrieving them, she placed them next to the others.

"All the lettering looks the same."

Casey held her flashlight closer. "Almost like a label."

"Here's one with A-N-T-I-C on it."

"Wait." Casey moved the pieces around. "What does that look like to you?"

Monah tried to sound it out. Then it came to her. "Atlantic Paper." She frowned. "That name is familiar." She tapped on her chin. "Where did I hear of that company?"

"Did some salesman come to the library trying to get you to switch to their product?"

Recollection started slowly then sped to a reckless dash through her mind. "Greg Dyer."

"What about him?"

Monah grasped Casey's arm. "I know where I saw the name. It was with Mike after we'd gone to the school for the first time for the minutes of their meetings. I had time to scan the notes while Mike drove me back to the library. Greg wanted the school to change from using Pine Mills Paper to Atlantic Paper."

Casey swung her light toward Monah's face. "Hold on. Just what are you thinking?"

Monah shook her head. "I'm not sure what to think. But isn't it odd that the warehouse he's supposed to be trying to sell has labels from the company he's been trying to push the school to use?"

Casey grabbed up the scraps of paper. "Let's go."

"Where?"

"Back to the library. I'd rather try to figure this out there. This place gives me the creeps."

Monah followed Casey out of the warehouse. Was it the place that made them skittish or the knowledge of what they'd found?

CHAPTER ⚏⚏ SEVENTEEN

A re you all right, Detective?"
　　 Mike blinked and closed his mouth, too late, he supposed, to keep the surprise from showing on his face.

Greg Dyer pulled his arm from around Dena Drolen's waist and gestured toward a crystal decanter sitting next to an ice bucket. "Can I get you something to drink?"

"Uh, no thanks. I'm fine." Grappling to regain his composure, Mike crossed the room and grasped Greg's proffered hand. "I didn't realize you and Mrs. Drolen were friends."

"More like business partners, really."

"Wayne and Greg were the ones with the business relationship," Dena inserted quickly, "but one could hardly call them partners. Just friends with similar interests." She shifted, adding inches to the breach growing between her and Greg. Her hands fluttered nervously, like two startled birds. "Greg just stopped by to offer his condolences."

Mike directed his attention to Greg. Unlike Dena, he looked calm, relaxed, at ease with himself and the situation. "Nice of you."

"Greg and I got acquainted through Wayne," Dena continued. "We've known each other for years." She laughed—too loudly.

Mike began taking mental notes of Dena's behavior. *Swallows repeatedly. Refuses to make eye contact.* His gaze dropped to the edge of her blouse where her fingers were plucking at the hem. *Fidgeting with her clothing.* She was hiding something.

"Why don't we sit down?" Greg took Dena by the shoulders and led her to a plush leather sofa. "You're tired. This has been a hard day."

"Yes," Dena agreed, sinking onto the cushions. "Very hard."

She sat, lips pursed, while Greg poured her a glass of water and pressed it into her hand.

"Drink up."

Tipping the glass obediently, she took a delicate sip. Though still flushed, she appeared more in control when at last she lowered the glass. "Thank you."

Greg shrugged. "No problem. Now"—he turned to Mike—"what can we do for you, Detective?"

"Actually, I just came by to check on Mrs. Drolen." He glanced at the new widow. Sometime between when she'd left the fundraiser and now, she'd changed into a plain silk blouse and black slacks. "If there's anything I can do, please don't hesitate to ask."

"I appreciate the offer." Fresh tears welled in her eyes, and she took another hasty sip from her glass.

Mike looked away. That was real pain he saw on her face, not feigned for his benefit. Still, where were all the people—friends and family giving support? The Drolens were a popular couple, which should have meant lots of visitors. He tucked the question away for later and looked at Greg. "So, tell me about this business relationship. How did you and Wayne meet?"

Greg slithered—there wasn't any other way to describe it—around the couch and sat near Dena. "Won't you have a seat, Detective?"

Mike took the chair he indicated, near enough to read any

subtle communication that passed between the two.

"Wayne and I went way back, before I got involved with real estate." Greg made himself comfortable with his legs crossed and arms draping the back of the couch. "As a matter of fact, we worked together on the renovation of a housing project a few years ago. I found the land, and he came up with the funding."

"Really."

Greg nodded. "Apart from that, there've been small things, you know, just quick little ventures here and there. Nothing major but profitable."

"I see."

"Yep. I told Dena here, she won't have a thing to worry about, moneywise. Wayne saw to that."

And yet they'd been arguing. Careful to maintain his casual posture, Mike studied the real estate agent. Just why had he thought it necessary to reveal that bit of information? "I'm glad to hear it, for Mrs. Drolen's sake."

The phone on the coffee table rang. Dena made no move toward it, and her face remained impassive. Greg got up to answer. "Hello?" He paused to listen. "Yes, hello, Mrs. Wright."

The mayor's wife. It was to be expected that she would call.

"No, I'm sorry, she's not accepting visitors today. Yes, I'll be sure to pass along your condolences." He pointed at the phone, his brows raised in question, but when Dena shook her head, he returned to the conversation. "No, there's nothing anyone can do at the moment. To be honest, we're asking that people refrain from calling or coming by until Dena's had a chance to make the necessary arrangements." Another pause. "That's right—her family will be arriving in the morning. Uh-huh. Okay. I'll tell her."

That explained the lack of visitors, but why was Greg the one assisting her? Too many unanswered questions.

"Thanks for calling, Mrs. Wright. You take care, too." Greg hung up and passed a slip of paper on which he'd written the Wrights' phone number to Dena. "You probably already have this, but I took it down just in case."

Her hand shook as she grasped the note. "Thanks."

Mike cleared his throat. "Mrs. Drolen, I do have a few questions for you—if you feel up to it, that is."

Eyes wary, she looked at him then at Greg, who moved to stand at her shoulder. "Okay."

Elbows propped on his knees, Mike handed her a tissue from the coffee table. "First, I'd like to know a little about Mr. Drolen's health history. Did he have any kind of heart trouble that you're aware of, any health issues that might explain his sudden collapse?"

Dena shook her head. "High cholesterol, maybe, but no heart problems."

"What about a stroke? Any history of that in his family?"

Again Dena shook her head, and Greg joined her. "Wayne and I used to run together. Three miles every day. He was as healthy as me." He patted his lean stomach.

"Did he drink or take medications?" Mike continued.

"No, which is why none of this makes sense." Her voice broke on the last.

Greg's hand moved to her shoulder. "It's okay, Dena." Uncomfortable silence broken only by her quiet sniffling followed. Greg looked at Mike. "This may not be the best time for your questions, Detective, so unless you have anything to report—"

As if on cue, Mike's cell phone jangled. He took one look at the caller ID and motioned toward the hall. "Mind if I take this out there?"

Dena nodded. "Go right ahead."

Mike walked from the room and flipped the phone open. "Brockman."

"You were right." Excitement colored Ted Levy's voice. "He was poisoned."

Mike tossed a quick glance over his shoulder. Dena still sat on the couch. Greg leaned over and spoke into her ear. Mike lowered his voice. "That was quick."

"It was easy, considering I already knew what to look for."

"You mean. . . ?"

"Monkshood. Same as Charlotte Tait. We've got us a second murder."

The news hardly made him feel better. He almost hated to ask. "Any idea how the poison got into his system?"

"Ingested. There are still traces in his stomach. I didn't even have to do a full autopsy. Just went straight to the source."

Suddenly, the image of Wayne Drolen's half-consumed bottle of water spun crazily in Mike's mind. It was still in his glove compartment. Right where he left it after he found out Monah had given it to Wayne.

"Okay, write me up a full report. And Ted, I've got a water bottle I'm going to need you to analyze."

Behind him, the sound of Dena's glass dropping on the tiled floor shattered the silence.

~

Monah stacked the unsold books from the fund-raiser onto the cart and then shoved the empty box under the counter with more force than necessary. She and Casey had planned to investigate a couple more burned buildings, in the daylight this time, but since Jamie called in sick—again—Monah had to fill in for her. Jamie's sick days were adding up lately. Did the girl want a job or not?

After finishing a double mocha latte for the much-needed

caffeine, Monah pushed the cart from behind the counter. The bell above the door chimed, but Monah was already heading toward the shelves and didn't turn to see who'd come in. She wasn't in the mood to be cheery.

"Monah Trenary! I thought you were my friend."

The shrill voice stalled Monah's steps. Dena stood at the counter, her eyes red and swollen. Monah rushed to her side and clasped Dena's hand.

"I am your friend, Dena. Why would you say such a thing?"

Dena shook free of Monah's grasp and moved back. "Liar! You killed my husband."

Monah's mouth sagged open. All around them, people stared. She tried to lead Dena to the office for privacy, but Dena shoved her away.

"Get your hands off me."

The venom in her voice shook Monah to her very core. "I didn't kill Wayne. What makes you think that?"

"I don't think it. I know it. Detective Brockman said as much."

Monah slumped against the counter. Mike told her that? Why?

Dena leaned in until their faces were mere inches apart. "He said you poisoned Wayne. You put it in his water." Her lips curled back in a snarl. "Thank goodness I didn't drink the bottle you gave me, or I'd be lying in the morgue alongside my husband." Tears filled her eyes. "How dare you!"

Monah didn't see the hand aimed at her face until it was too late. The crack of the slap stabbed her eardrum at the same time her cheek exploded with pain. Tears blurred her vision, but she still managed to see Dena's hand coming at her again. Arms raised, she braced to fend off the blow, but it never came. Mike held Dena by the wrists.

"Mrs. Drolen, I never said Monah killed your husband. I only said the water bottle would be part of the investigation."

Dena jerked her hands loose. "How else did poison get into Wayne's body if not through the water that she"—she pointed accusingly at Monah—"gave him?"

Poison? Wayne died from being poisoned like Miss Tait? The confirmation didn't provide nearly the satisfaction Monah expected.

Mike angled himself between Monah and Dena. "I'm asking you to go home, Mrs. Drolen. Let me do my job."

"Well, you'd better get busy arresting someone." Dena's whole body shook as she glared at Monah. "And I suggest you start with her."

"I'll handle it." Mike's voice dropped to a low and gentle tone as he led her to the door. "Go on home now. You still have plans to make, and the next couple of days will be tough for you. I'll get in touch when I know something."

The door hadn't even closed completely before Mike returned to the spot where Monah stood rooted. "Are you okay?"

She nodded.

"Are you sure?" He touched her cheek, his gaze warm with concern.

Monah swallowed a sudden lump in her throat. "I'll be fine."

"Okay." Mike drew a breath and shoved his hands into his pockets. "I need you to close the library."

She blinked, momentarily unable to decipher the events and information of the past few minutes. "Close? For how long?"

"At least the rest of the day." He stepped to the office door. "Gather your things, Sandy. You have the rest of the day off." He didn't wait for questions or arguments but faced the people gaping at him. "I'm sorry, folks, but I'm going to have to ask that you clear the library."

Mike waved Sandy over and herded her and the handful of patrons toward the door, easily avoiding the need to answer their questions. As Mike continued guiding the people out, Monah tried to fathom what had happened since yesterday that had him acting so businesslike she barely recognized him. He wouldn't even look her in the eyes. Maybe if he did, she might be able to understand. . .something.

Two officers entered. One remained at the door. The other followed Mike toward the office. "Start at the desk. I'll be with you in a minute."

He waited until the officer was inside the office before he turned to Monah. For the first time, their eyes met but only for a moment. Long enough for her to see. . . Anger? Regret? Guilt?

Her trembling legs carried her only as far as the nearest chair. She dropped onto the seat with a hard *thud*. Dena's slap may have hurt, but it was nothing compared to the sledgehammer the look in Mike's eyes had slammed into her heart. "What's going on?"

He ran his hand over his face. "You have to leave, Monah."

"Why? What happened?"

He pulled some papers from his pocket. "These warrants give me permission to search the library again." He held one of them out to her, his eyes only making it to her chin. "And this one is for your laptop."

"My. . .my laptop?" Her heart ached from beating so hard. "Talk to me, Mike. Why are you doing this?"

His throat worked hard enough to make his Adam's apple bob like a yo-yo. "I can't talk to you about the case anymore, Monah. I could lose my job for conferring with a suspect."

CHAPTER EIGHTEEN

Mike watched silently as Monah left the library. Officer Crowley closed the door behind her and locked it. "Your orders, sir?"

Mike's mouth felt like sandpaper. His heart. . . Well, he refused to think too hard on the pain he'd read in Monah's eyes. That couldn't be an act. Nobody was that good, right? She had to be innocent, regardless of what Ted Levy's report said. Drolen's water had been poisoned—that much he knew. He also knew it couldn't have been done by Monah.

Frustration gnawed at his gut. "Check the back," he ground out. "Concentrate on the storage rooms. Let me know what you find. Parker, do a sweep of Ms. Trenary's office and desk. The laptop—bring that to me. I want to go over it myself."

Parker returned too quickly with the computer. At the eagerness on his face, Mike flushed with anger. "Forget it. I'm checking this thing myself."

At least he wasn't stupid. Without argument, Parker turned and entered the office. Through the window, Mike saw him begin meticulously sorting through the files stacked on the desk. Whatever his other faults, Parker was exceptionally good at his job.

Drawing a breath, Mike took the computer to one of the

round library tables and sat down. He lifted the cover. The computer booted in minutes. No password. How like Monah to be so trusting.

The thought forced him, stumbling, to his feet. He couldn't do it. He refused to believe there was anything to be found there. *God, help me.* He sighed and rubbed his hands over his face. Maybe the laptop could wait.

He circled to the counter where he'd seen Monah store flats of water on more than one occasion. As before, several bottles stood lined and ready, their seals unbroken. He took one out and lifted it to the fluorescent lighting overhead. It looked normal. He'd ask Ted to examine one just in case. He moved a second bottle aside. Rummaging sounded from the storage room across from the bathrooms.

"Anything, Crowley?" Mike said.

"Not yet. Lots of boxes back here though. Doesn't that woman throw anything away?"

He obviously didn't know Monah. "Keep looking." Mike glanced toward the office window. Parker had moved from the desk to the filing cabinet. His back was to the door.

Squatting in front of the shelf, Mike pulled the remaining water bottles from the shelf and set them on the floor. From the back of the shelf, a long white envelope, partially crumpled, stuck out, blank and menacing. Hand over his mouth, Mike studied it silently. What was it doing there? Did he really want to know? Something in his brain screamed no.

Do your job, Brockman.

His voice rattled inside his head. He retrieved a pair of latex gloves from his pocket, tugged them on, and reached for the envelope. It wasn't sealed. Careful to avoid touching too much of the envelope, he gently lifted the flap.

Seeds.

Mike's stomach slammed to his toes. He didn't have to wonder what kind. He'd been studying monkshood too much not to recognize the incriminating evidence in his hand. He fought back a rush of agonized disbelief and slid the envelope, seeds and all, into a plastic bag that he took from his jacket pocket. Knees shaking, he rose to his feet. There had to be an explanation. He'd bring Monah in for questioning, she would come up with some zany excuse for why there were monkshood seeds at the desk in the library, and they would all get back to life as normal.

"Whatcha got there, Detective?" Parker's eyes gleamed with interest.

Mike jerked his head up. He'd been so absorbed he hadn't even noticed Parker watching. "You finished in there?"

"No, sir, but I thought maybe you could use some help." Parker gestured to the bag. "That what I think it is?"

"Depends on what you think it is."

"Monkshood seeds? That's what the ME thinks did Drolen and Miss Tait in, right?"

Mike laid the bag on the counter and folded his arms. "Just how do you know that, Parker?"

"Easy." Crowley emerged from the back. "Word around the station is they were poisoned. Hate to tell you, Detective—it's common knowledge."

Small towns. They certainly had their shortcomings. Mike grunted and shoved off the counter. "Nothing's definite until we've gathered all of the evidence, including"—his gaze swung to rest on Parker—"anything else you might find in the office. Now, get to work. You, too, Crowley."

He hated barking orders, but the way his insides felt, they were lucky it wasn't worse. The officers returned to their investigation.

Mike labeled the bag then went back to the laptop. He'd have to search it now.

Opening Monah's documents, he quickly began scrolling the list. They were organized alphabetically, by type. Feeling as though he might be sick, he read through the names, settling on a few, skimming the rest.

Assault—Blunt Object
Fingerprinting
Human Decomposition
Manslaughter—Vehicular

His breath caught as he stumbled upon the most damaging of all—*Poisoning*.

~

Monah sat in the interrogation room facing the wall with the big mirror. They might as well post a sign saying WE ARE WATCHING YOU above it. She couldn't look at her reflection. Doing so might bring on the tears she'd been fighting, and she wouldn't give her "viewers" the pleasure of seeing her fall apart.

Who all was back there? Was Mike one of the observers? Would he be the one asking the questions? He would be easier to face than any of the others, but did she ever want to see him again? Why couldn't he have just asked his questions in the library parking lot where he found her waiting for him? Why did he insist on an interrogation at the station where anyone could scrutinize her every word and movement? Most of all, why couldn't he believe in her innocence?

Monah checked her watch. Was Casey here yet? The first call she'd made when Mike told her to head to the station was to Casey, begging her to meet her there. The second call was to her mother. Monah would need all the prayers she could get. Not only would Mom pray without ceasing, but she'd also run to the station to offer comfort and support. Needing to know if someone she cared about had arrived, she pulled out her cell phone.

The door opened. Officer Parker stood in the opening. "Calling someone?"

Yep. They were watching, just waiting for her to make a move before they made theirs. Police were so predictable. "Not anymore."

"Were you calling Miss Alexander?"

How did he know that? "Exactly why am I here?" If he could be businesslike, so could she. Even if it killed her.

Parker slid out a chair, sat down, and set a folder on the table. He lifted the cover and pulled out a clear plastic bag marked Evidence. "These were found on the shelf under the counter at the library. Can you explain why they were there?"

She reached for the bag to get a better look then stopped. "Can I—"

He shrugged. "Sure. Just don't open it."

The black objects were so tiny that Monah had to hold the bag close in order to get a good view. "What are they?" She adjusted her glasses and squinted. "Seeds?"

Parker rested his forearms on the table. "Monkshood seeds, to be exact."

"Monks—" She threw the bag on the table. Monkshood was the reason Mike had removed all the gardening books from the library. "I have no idea how they got there."

Parker returned the bag to the folder then laced his fingers. "Sandy, you, and Jamie are the only people allowed behind the counter, correct?"

So they'd narrowed the suspect list. Too bad they'd narrowed it to the wrong three. "We're the only ones who are *supposed* to be back there."

"You're saying others have been behind the counter?"

"I'm saying it's not unusual to find that some people have wandered back there."

"Like who?"

Oh man. Great time to draw a blank. "Ah—"

"Why are the files 'Assault,' 'Manslaughter,' and 'Poisoning' saved on your laptop?"

All the air in the room vanished. Forming words was no longer possible. How was she supposed to answer that?

Parker didn't give her time to think. "You have information about human decomposition. Why would you need to know that?"

Think, Monah. "I study criminology." *Stupid answer.*

He frowned. "Why?"

Breathe. "Don't you find it interesting?"

"I do. But why should you? You're not in law enforcement."

"No, but my boyfriend is."

Parker sat back in his chair, mouth agape. Now he knew what it felt like to be put on the spot.

She leaned forward and looked him in the eyes. "I haven't done anything wrong. I haven't killed anyone, nor do I ever intend to do so."

The corners of his mouth twitched just a fraction. "All right. I think we're through here for now. Make sure I'm able to reach you if I have any further questions." Standing, he waited at the door then held it open for her.

Outside, Mike caught her arm as she moved past. "Are you okay?"

Monah nodded.

"I don't know that I'll ever figure you out," he whispered for her ears alone.

She forced herself not to react. Spotting Casey pacing in the hall, Monah rushed to her. After they embraced, Casey held her at arm's length. "Are you all right?"

"Yeah, I'm fine. A little shaken but okay."

Monah turned to ask Mike if she was free to go and heard an officer say "password-protected file" and "laptop." He went on to add "Brandy Purcell." Monah's heart froze. They'd found her secret files.

CHAPTER ⚏⚏ NINETEEN

B randy who?" Puzzled, Mike stared at the words scribbled on a Post-it note. "What in the world is *Death Spiral*?" He pointed at the next line down. "And that. What is that? *Murder to a Tee?* What is all this, Crowley?"

Behind them, Casey squeaked.

Mike turned. She stood with her fingers pressed to her mouth. Next to her, Monah's eyes were wide. . .and horrified.

He stepped closer to her. "Monah, can you explain what these files mean? Why did you try to hide them?"

"I. . .I. . ." Her long hair rustled as she shook her head.

Casey started hopping, her hands fluttering. "Brandy Purcell! You know, the True-Life Detective series? *Death Spiral* was her biggest seller."

Tearing his gaze from Casey, Mike pressed toward Monah. "I don't get it. Why do you have this stuff on your laptop?" Concerned that she might not answer, he instilled pleading in his gaze and lowered his voice. "What's going on, Monah? Are you going to need a lawyer? Tell me right now if you do. I don't want you to say anything that might incriminate you."

"A lawyer?" Instantly, Casey stopped hopping. "Why would she need a lawyer?" She swung to Monah. "Why *do* you have Brandy Purcell's books on your computer?"

The entire station had gone quiet. Even the aging copier, normally loud as it clacked out copies, fell silent. Maybe somebody unplugged it. Or possibly it had finally given up the ghost. They'd have to call a repairman in the morning.

The randomness of the idea struck Mike as absurd. How could he be thinking about copiers when Monah stood in front of him looking small and vulnerable and completely terrified? His heart thumped painfully. Then and there, he knew he'd do whatever it took to protect her, even if it meant turning in his gun and badge.

He touched her arm. "It's okay. I'm right here, sweetheart, and whatever this note"—he waved the Post-it—"means, we'll work it out together. I just need you to be honest with me."

God, please let her have a reasonable answer for all of this. Please, Lord. All I ask is for her to have a reasonable *answer.*

She stared up into his gaze through several long seconds then moistened her lips. Her jaw worked, and she opened her mouth. "I'm. . ." She took a breath. "I'm Brandy Purcell."

That wasn't it. His heart sank.

"I mean, I'm not really Brandy Purcell. I write Brandy Purcell. I'm the author."

"You're what?" Monah's mother stood with her hand frozen on the door.

"Mom." Monah's face went ashen. "I can explain."

Casey shrieked then slapped Monah's arm. "Why didn't you say anything? Do you know how awesome this is? Oh my gosh, *ohmygosh!* My best friend is Brandy Purcell. Did you write all of her books? When does the next one come out? Is that why you had all those files on your laptop? 'Cuz that was a little spooky, you know. In fact, if that's not the reason, I'm gonna have to find a new best friend. I mean, 'stalker' just isn't on my list of top ten people to hang out with. Holy smoke, Monah, I sound like you."

"Not exactly, Casey," Mrs. Trenary said softly. She left the door and walked over to Monah, her face a mixture of disappointment and sorrow. "Monah never told me as much as you did just now."

Mike jumped in before Casey could gain her second wind. "Why don't we step back into my office? Monah's got a lot of explaining to do, and I'd rather she not do it out here. Mrs. Trenary, I'm afraid I'm going to need a few minutes alone with your daughter, if that's all right."

Always dignified, Mrs. Trenary gave a small nod before reaching out to grasp Monah's hand. "We'll talk after."

Monah's gaze swung over the stunned faces of the gathered officers. She gave a quick nod. Mike clasped her elbow and led her past Lois, the station dispatcher, who was rummaging too earnestly inside her desk. If she was digging for a pen. . .

Sure enough, Lois gave a snort of exclamation and held up a fine-point Sharpie. "Ms. Trenary, could I get—"

"Save it, Lois," Mike barked. An autograph? The woman wanted an autograph. Unbelievable. His gaze swept the station. "The rest of you, get back to work."

On cue, the officers erupted into motion, though several of them still eyed Monah curiously, Parker and Crowley included.

Inside his office, Mike closed the door, shutting out the busy hum. Returning to his battered desk, he sat on the edge and gazed at Monah steadily. "Now, are you gonna tell me what's going on?"

He'd prepared himself for the worst. He'd fought through all the emotions of watching Monah sit alone and afraid while she awaited questioning and prepared himself to appear calm, professional. He'd even prepared for the possibility that the woman he loved more dearly than life might be involved in a murder.

He wasn't prepared for her to burst into tears.

Devastated, Monah lowered her face into her hands and sobbed. The pain in her mom's eyes played through her mind. She'd hurt her mom, the very thing she'd tried to avoid all these years.

"Hey." Mike knelt beside her and brushed back her hair. "Talk to me, Monah. Tell me what's wrong."

The tenderness in his voice made her want to cry harder. Did he have any idea how much she loved him or how much he'd wounded her with his distrust?

"Is it the warrant? I hated doing that, you know."

Taking a deep breath, Monah struggled to pull herself together. A tissue appeared in her line of vision. She looked up as she took it. Affection beamed from Mike's eyes, soothing some of her pain. Stalling, she slowly mopped her face. Mike didn't say a word but let her take her time. And now she needed to explain.

"I tried so hard to keep her from finding out so she wouldn't be hurt."

Mike pulled the other chair close. "Who?"

Monah's throat burned as she fought more tears. "Mom." She took two deep breaths to control her emotions. "You know I'm adopted."

Mike nodded.

"When I graduated and started working full-time at the library, I had a lot of time alone after I locked up." She dabbed at her eyes. "My curiosity about my birth mother grew so strong, I started researching. I figured as long as Mom and Dad didn't find out, no harm could come from learning something about my roots."

He dipped his head into her view. "Why do I get the feeling what you learned wasn't all that pretty?"

She lifted her head to meet his gaze. "She was a drug dealer and addict." She tapped her glasses. "I always figured my poor eyesight was because of her drug abuse." She shrugged. "From what I understand, the Boston police knew her quite well because of all the petty theft arrests among. . .other things. She wasn't always like that. She grew up in a well-to-do area."

The old resentment of shuffling from one foster home to another rose. She tamped the feeling down. "I know this is a story you've heard hundreds of times. At first, I hated learning I was one of those statistics. Then I started thinking about why that number grew."

Mike took her hand in his. "Hence your study of criminology."

She nodded, enjoying the comfort of his touch. "That's how it started. When I began writing mysteries, the research intensified."

He smiled. "And here I thought it was because of me."

Her heart lightened. "Would it help if I told you I appreciate you more?"

He laughed and squeezed her hand. "It helps." He ran his thumb along the corner of her eye and wiped away the last tear. "So, how did all this lead you into writing these"—he glanced at his notes—"Brandy Purcell novels?"

"The need to make the world better." She refolded the tissue and laid it on her leg. "It was too late to help my birth mother, keep her from making mistakes, but I thought maybe I could help others by using stories. You know, trying to right wrongs, seeking justice, maybe pointing some young people in the right direction."

"And your detective stories do that?"

She looked down, slightly embarrassed. "They may be fiction, but if in some small way they affect the real world, then I've accomplished my goal."

"But you never told your mom."

She curled her hands into fists. "I couldn't. You see, I named the main character after my birth mother because I never thought the books would become as popular as they are. Once the series took off, there was no way of telling Mom without revealing what I'd done. We never talked about where I came from. I thought it was because it bothered my parents so much."

"And now?"

Aching with guilt, she shrugged again. "I don't know why I wanted to find out who my birth mother was. I love Mom. We're so close it's as though she's the one who gave birth to me." She shook her head. "I was so stupid. If I'd told her of my curiosity from the very beginning, she probably would have helped me. But I hid it and then compounded the problem by hiding my writing. And now I've hurt her more than I would have by coming clean."

Mike clasped her chin with his fingers. "There's no time like the present. I can promise she won't stop loving you. She may shed some tears"—he smiled and lifted the tissue from her leg to her eyes—"but her love for you runs deep."

And Monah's love for Mike just deepened. She smiled. "Thank you." About to stand, she changed her mind and gazed at him once again. "Do you still question my innocence?"

He met her eyes. "Not a bit. I'm sorry I doubted you at all. The evidence—"

"Yeah, I know. I'd have thought the same thing under the circumstances." Monah paused. "The seeds?"

Mike shook his head. "Circumstantial. We'll keep it on file but only because we have to. I've always known you aren't the killer." He stood and reached for the doorknob. "Go and talk to your mom. I'll be praying. . .for both of you."

"Thanks. I appreciate that."

He opened the door, and Monah stood face-to-face with her mother.

CHAPTER ⚟ TWENTY

Monah drove to her mom's house, her heart switching between racing and stalling. Her mom led the way. Monah hoped she wasn't crying. By the look in her eyes when they left Mike's office, the worry and pain her mom endured was more than she could bear.

Lord, help me make it right. Help me prove how sorry I am and how much I love her.

Monah got caught at the town's one light. Her mom had already arrived and entered the quaint, single-story ranch house by the time Monah pulled in the driveway. She walked inside. Glasses clattered in the kitchen. She followed the sound. Her mom held out a glass filled with ice.

"What would you like to drink? Tea? Water?"

In just a few steps, Monah crossed the room. "I'm so sorry, Mom." The tears were already flowing from both of them. "I never meant to hurt you. I was so stupid." Monah grasped her mom's hands. "Please forgive me."

Her mom set the glasses aside and pulled Monah into her arms. "I love you, dear. Of course I forgive you." They stood weeping for several minutes before getting their tears under control.

Monah leaned back to look in her mom's eyes. "I'd like to explain."

"You don't have to, Monah. I'm sure you have good reasons."

She shook her head. "That's just it. I thought my reasoning was sound years ago. Now I know I could have gone to you with any and all of my questions."

She took her mom's hand and led her into the living room. They shared the sofa as always, sitting close like best friends confiding hopes and dreams. She spent the next half hour revealing all she'd done to find her birth mother, all she'd discovered, and her pitiful reasons for keeping it all a secret.

Her mom finally nodded. "Your father and I decided not to mention much, planning to leave it up to you whether or not you wanted details. At the time, we thought it best. Now I wonder if it was a mistake." She twined her fingers with Monah's. "I wish you'd come to me."

"I thought it would hurt you, and I never wanted that to happen. In my lack of wisdom, I ended up hurting you more. I'm so sorry."

"Enough apologizing." She tucked a stray strand of hair behind Monah's ear. "I love you, Monah. Nothing could ever change that. I may not have given birth to you, but I feel like we have one heart, as though we're connected by something stronger than any cord."

"Aw, Mom." Monah wrapped her arms around her mother's neck. "I hope you know how much I love you."

"I know." Sniffing, she wiped away Monah's tears. "I know."

Monah pulled a tissue from the box on the coffee table and blew her nose. "Why do you suppose God allowed all this to happen? The suspicion and evidence against me, I mean. I would never consider doing anything so awful."

Her mom propped her elbow on the back of the couch and rested her head against the palm of her hand. "We can never presume to know the depths of God's thoughts or plans. We can only trust that He has our best interests at heart." She shrugged, and a tiny smile curved her mouth. "It did make you confess your secret to me." She squeezed Monah's hand. "So when do I get to start bragging that my daughter is the famous Brandy Purcell?"

"I'm not famous. And I didn't figure you even knew anything about those books. You've never checked them out of the library."

Her smile fading, Monah's mom stood and crossed to the rolltop desk. Monah had always avoided the desk because her mom had cautioned her so often when she was little that all her "important" papers were stored there. She pulled a key from one of the drawers and opened the desk. The True-Life Detective series lined one shelf.

"Mom! You never told me you read those."

She made a face. "I was a little embarrassed. I never wanted to confess that when a new book was released, I'd hole up for as long as it took to finish it." She propped one hand on her hip as she closed the cabinet door. "You know, you write entirely too slow. One a month would suffice."

Monah's mouth dropped open to protest. Her mom laughed before plopping back beside her on the couch. "I'm addicted, that's all."

Shouting from outside the living room window drew Monah's attention. She shifted to look out. Mr. Sparks stood, his arms akimbo, while Mrs. Sparks shook a fistful of flowers in his direction.

Monah chuckled. "They still can't get along in the garden, can they? They've been like that for as long as I can remember."

"You'd think they hated each other, but they're just so sweet and loving. . .when they're anywhere *but* the garden."

Monah knew better than to listen to someone else's

conversation, but she tucked her hair behind her ear to hear more clearly.

"Why would you put a poisonous plant in our garden?" Mrs. Sparks's shrill voice pierced the air. "You want to get sick? Or worse yet, do you want to kill me?"

Heart hammering, Monah leaned over the back of the couch for a better look. Her mom smacked her backside.

"Monah, stop eavesdropping. I taught you better than that."

Monah pointed out the window. "What kind of flower is that, Mom? Can you tell?"

Mom scooted beside her. "Purple. Hmm. I wonder—"

"Monkshood?" Monah stood. "I'm going to talk to them." Ignoring her mother's protests, she headed out the back door, followed closely by her mom. "Hello, Mr. and Mrs. Sparks. How've you two been?"

The couple stopped hollering long enough to greet her then included her in their argument. "Can you believe this, Monah?" Mr. Sparks stomped to her side and motioned toward his wife. "She yanked out all those beautiful flowers just because they contain poison. Don't you think the two of us are old enough to know to leave them alone? But she thinks I'm trying to kill her."

Mrs. Sparks moved to her other side. "Anyone in their right mind would know not to plant something poisonous in the first place."

"Now you think I'm not in my right mind? Is there anything you like about me, woman?"

Monah fought a laugh and slipped her arms through each of theirs. "Stop it, you two. You know as much as I do how much you love each other. Now kiss and make up."

She pushed them together. They hemmed and hawed for a moment before tiny smiles turned to full-blown grins. Mr. Sparks pulled his wife into his arms, swung her around, and planted a kiss on her lips.

"I'm sorry, sweets. I should have asked you first."

Mrs. Sparks tugged off her gloves, tossed them to the ground, and placed her hands on his cheeks. "I can never stay mad at you long. You're the dearest man I know." She pulled his head down for another kiss.

Monah peeked at her mom. She had her hand over her mouth, but it didn't hide the way her shoulders shook as she laughed. Monah had to break the couple up, or she'd never get to ask her questions.

"Hey, you two."

They didn't hear her. Or they ignored her.

"Mr. and Mrs. Sparks."

As though pulled from a daze, they turned to her. "Yes?"

"Could I ask what kind of flower it was you two were fighting about?"

Mr. Sparks's eyebrows raised. "You're not trying to get me back into trouble, are you, Monah?"

"No, sir. I wouldn't do that. I've recently gotten interested in plants and wondered what you had that was so dangerous."

Mrs. Sparks replaced her gloves and lifted the purple plants from the ground where she'd thrown them. "It's monkshood, dear. Wolfsbane. Very poisonous. Oh, don't touch it," she said, stopping Monah before she actually grasped the stem. "The poison can be absorbed through your skin."

Monah turned to Mr. Sparks. "Did you go out and buy this plant or the seeds?"

He rocked on his heels, arms behind his back. "The seeds were given to us along with several other types. All part of belonging to the local garden club."

These two belonged to a garden club? Together? Monah hoped they behaved themselves at the meetings.

She frowned. "A local club? Does that mean that every member received the same sets of seeds?"

Mrs. Sparks slipped her arm around Monah's and led her to the edge of the garden. "That's right, dear. Each year, the board decides on five different varieties of plants and sends its members the seed packets." She pointed to a row near the center. "Those are what we received this year. Pretty, aren't they?"

"They sure are, Mrs. Sparks." Monah glanced at her mom. "Who all is on the board that makes those decisions?"

"Oh my." Mrs. Sparks motioned her husband closer. "Who are the board members, Clarence? Do you remember?"

"One works at the school. Has a strange name."

Bells rang loud and clear in Monah's head. "Simone Wallace."

Mr. Sparks snapped his fingers. "That's it." He shook his head. "Strange name."

"Who else? Do you remember?"

The couple narrowed their eyes and peered at the sky. Then Mrs. Sparks shrugged. "Sorry, dear. They're just not coming to me. I could go in the house and look at one of the flyers."

Monah had no idea how long that would take, and she was anxious to do a little more digging. "You can look for it later, Mrs. Sparks. Give it to Mom when you find it. She can call me with the list of names. And thanks for your help."

She gave her mom a hug then headed into the house for her purse and keys. Excitement raced through her. She had a strong lead and couldn't wait to find out more. First she'd call Casey and have her meet her at the library. Then she'd swing by the police station and retrieve her laptop. If Mike told the truth about believing in her innocence, he shouldn't need it any longer.

CHAPTER TWENTY-ONE

A men."
Mike lifted his head, his heart considerably lighter than it'd been when he first bowed to pray. This case was wearing on his nerves—and his peace. It was time to find the real killer so he and Monah could put all of this behind them.

The aroma of freshly brewed coffee wafted from a Styrofoam cup on the corner of his desk. Monah had brought it on her way to work. Now that he'd finished the investigation of the library, there'd been no reason to keep it closed, and she couldn't have been happier. Mike couldn't be happier, as he took a sip from the cup, that the tension between them had faded.

He smiled, remembering the jewelry store he'd walked past a couple of weekends ago and the diamond solitaire glinting in the window. His leather chair creaked as he leaned back to lace his fingers behind his head. Someday he'd slip a ring just like that onto Monah's finger. He pictured her face, the way her dark eyes would light up when she saw it. But first. . .

He straightened and snatched the Drolen file off his desk. Monah said only she, Jamie Canon, and Sandy Magrew were allowed behind the library counter. Since Monah couldn't be the killer, he'd have to investigate deeper into other suspects, and he knew just where to start.

"I'm heading to the library, Parker," Mike called. Grabbing his keys and shoulder holster, he returned Parker's brief nod before swinging through the door.

Sandy was putting the finishing touches on a display near the door when he arrived. "Good afternoon, Detective Brockman. What I can do for you today?" she said, straightening up.

Mike did a quick scan of the library. Except for a woman playing with a small boy in the children's section, the place appeared vacant. Where were Monah and Jamie? "No help today?"

"Jamie took the day off, and Monah went down to the temp office to see if she could find some part-time help. She's been so upset with Jamie over the time she's missed. It has really put us in a bind." She sucked air through her teeth then lifted a plump hand to her mouth. "Guess you didn't need to know all that."

Mike smiled to set her at ease then gestured toward the counter. "Mind if we talk a minute?"

"Not at all." She picked up her box of supplies—scissors, tape, and an assortment of paper from what Mike could see—and bustled to the counter. "Now," she huffed as she bent to shove the box onto a shelf, "what'd you want to talk about?" She lowered the hinged section of the countertop then rested the upper half of her body on it.

Mike tapped the wooden top. "This, actually. Monah says only three people are allowed back there."

Sandy's head bobbed. "That's right. Only me, Monah, and Jamie."

He gestured toward the hinged section that lifted to allow people to pass through. "Does that lock?"

Blushing, Sandy fumbled behind the counter a moment until Mike heard a soft click. "Uh, yeah, but we hardly ever check it."

"So what's to keep just anyone from finding their way back there?"

"W–well," Sandy stammered, "it's not like we leave the library unattended. One of us is always here. We would see."

Over her shoulder, a thin plume of smoke circled lazily toward the ceiling. Mike pointed. "Is something burning?"

"Wha—?"

Sandy gasped and then dashed toward the office. Through the window, he watched her snatch a pot off a hot plate and toss the contents into the trash. Afterward, she shoved her foot into the wastebasket and proceeded to stomp the daylights out of the can.

"Need any help?" he called as he ducked under the hinged counter and leaned against it, arms crossed.

"I've got it," Sandy croaked, fanning the air under the smoke alarm with a sheaf of papers.

Mike counted to ten then ducked back under the counter. By the time Sandy returned, he stood in the same spot he'd occupied when she left. "Everything okay?"

"Fine," she said, coughing. "I forgot I'd set some tea on before I started with that display. A flush of embarrassment stole over her cheeks. "Guess it's a good thing you stopped by."

"Guess so." Mike shrugged. "So, you're sure no one could sneak behind the counter without you seeing, huh?"

"Absolutely." Her confidence returning, Sandy lifted her chin. "We're very careful about who we allow back here."

Mike hid a smile and withdrew a notebook from his jacket pocket. "Right. So tell me how long you've worked with Monah."

"Let's see, it must be about"—she tilted her head and stroked her bottom lip with her forefinger—"seven, eight years? Something like that. Hard to remember."

"And Jamie? This her first year?"

"Second. She worked last summer, too."

Mike jotted the information down. Without looking up, he asked, "What can you tell me about her?"

"Other than the fact that she's been sick most of the summer?"

Mike clicked his pen and replaced it inside his pocket. "That why she's been out?"

The gleam returned to Sandy's eyes, and she nodded. "I've sorta been wondering if she isn't. . .you know. . .in the family way."

"Excuse me?"

"Pregnant." Sandy lowered her voice and pitched forward conspiratorially. "She's got all the symptoms—nausea, fatigue, unhealthy pallor at times." She straightened up, and her glance darted around the library. "Of course, I haven't voiced that opinion to anyone but you."

Uh-huh. The notebook joined the pen inside Mike's pocket. "I appreciate you taking the time to talk to me." He directed a glance toward the mother and son who had finished making their selections and were headed toward the counter. "I won't take up any more of your time."

And he wouldn't, now that he'd proven without a doubt that just about anybody could've slipped behind the counter and planted the monkshood seeds. The question was, who?

~

Monah punched the library's number into her cell phone. Three rings. Four.

Poor Sandy. With only her working, she probably had more to do than answer the phone—and on Thursday, no less. In half an hour, she'd be inundated with mothers and their children for reading day. Monah felt like a dog for skipping out on her—

"Hello?"

"Sandy! I've got someone to help for the rest of the summer.

He should be showing up within the hour."

A huff made its way through the airwaves. "He?"

"Yes. Matt Collier."

"Matt? You mean, Matt—the star-athlete-of-the-high-school Matt? The one girls fawn over?"

Monah was glad Sandy couldn't see her grin. "That's the one."

"Why would he want to work at the library?"

"I didn't ask, but I'm almost certain he plans to use the time studying to bring his grades up. At least he'll be there to help." Monah turned into the lot of Luke Kerrigan's landscaping business. She smiled at Sandy's silence. "Think of it this way. Our patronage ought to grow tenfold from everyone coming in to see him."

Another huff. "Yes, and then we'll need to hire someone else just to handle all the girls swooning over our new help."

"Or it may make Jamie come in more often."

"Well, where are you? Aren't you coming in today? Or are you calling in sick, too? It better not be for the same reason as Jamie."

Monah's mind scrambled. "What's Jamie's reason? She told me she was sick. Did she give you symptoms?" *Don't gossip, Monah.* "Never mind, and no, I won't be in for a while. I'm taking a plant to the winner of our drawing from the fund-raiser."

Well, the second winner anyway. Monah and Casey decided to work through their suspect list to narrow the number that needed concentration. They wanted to question Robin Beck further about Miss Tait's death. After thinking about it, they decided using the guise of winning the drawing would be a good way to gather more information.

"Then, are you coming in?"

Sandy's high-pitched squeak spoke volumes. "No. I have one other stop to make. Then I'll be in. But don't worry. Matt will be there soon. Have him read to the children. Trust me. They'll love him." She didn't want to leave any time for arguing. "Gotta run." She hit the END button and tossed her phone into her purse.

Spotting Casey, Monah tamped down her feelings of guilt and opened the car door. "You ready?"

Casey waved and entered the building. A minute later, she emerged with Luke following her, a large potted plant in his arms. He opened the passenger door of Monah's car for Casey to get in then closed it behind her. Then he opened the back door and climbed in with the plant.

Monah stared at him in the rearview mirror. "You're going with us to the Becks'?"

Luke grinned. "Hi, Monah. Good to see you, too."

She made a face. "Why are you going?"

"I donated the plant. Gotta stand by my craft." He leaned up between the seats. "Unlike some so-called author pal of mine who didn't bother telling her friends she was a famous writer."

Monah rolled her eyes. "I'm not famous."

Casey looked at her over her sunglasses. "Maybe you would be if you weren't hiding."

Pulling her door closed, Monah reached for her seat belt and belted herself in. "All right, so we're all going to Robin's house. Great. Let's get going."

Luke leaned closer. "You're still hiding."

Monah shrugged. "I admit I was only putting off the inevitable by not telling my mom about the books. But we talked, and all is well now."

"Good." Casey squeezed her hand. "So, does that mean I can tell everyone?"

"Sure, but you'll have to stand in line. I think Mom's been burning the phones up spreading the news." She peered into the mirror. Luke stared back. "What?"

"Any other secrets?"

"Like what?"

He raised his brows. "Like, are you one of those maniacs who live out their books in real life?"

Monah looked away and started the engine. She reached for the gear shift, and Luke leaned forward and put his hand over hers.

"Monah?" Incredulity colored Luke's voice.

She turned to face him. "Sort of."

"What's that supposed to mean?"

Casey grabbed her arm. "You know karate, don't you? You've taken special driving classes, haven't you?"

Monah grinned.

"I knew it!" Casey screeched.

"I can't believe it." Luke was shaking his head. "I don't know you at all."

"Sure you do. You just don't know Brandy."

This time Monah managed to put the car in gear and headed back through town. In minutes they pulled into the Becks' driveway. She turned to Casey. "You know what you're going to say?"

Casey's mouth dropped open. "I thought you were doing the talking. I'm just here for support."

"Yeah, supporting me by doing the talking."

"You're the detective."

Luke put his hands on their shoulders. "Ladies. Why don't we just go in and congratulate her on winning one of my fabulous plants? I'm sure you'll come up with something by then."

Luke led the way, proudly holding his plant, and rang the bell. Lauren opened the door.

"Mom won? She'll be thrilled. She loves plants and flowers." She opened the door wider and waved them inside. "In fact, she's working in her garden right now. Come on. I'll let you surprise her."

They passed through the living room. Notes, pictures, and paperwork were strewed across the floor.

"Excuse the mess," Lauren said, motioning to the clutter. "It's my first year teaching, and I want to be ready."

Monah exchanged a glance with Casey. "You must be excited. You still have almost two months to go before school starts."

Lauren grinned as she opened the back door. "You have no idea. I think I've always wanted to be a teacher. I'm finally fulfilling my dream."

Monah forced a smile, reserving judgment. "Well, congratulations on your accomplishment."

"Thanks." She let the door slam behind them. "Mom, you have company."

Robin looked up from her kneeling position, dirt smudges on her face, and smiled. "Hi. To what do I owe this surprise?"

Luke moved from behind them and held out his plant, his buttons nearly bursting with the pride coloring his voice. "You won this from the drawing at the fund-raiser the other day."

"Oh wow! I never win anything." Robin rushed to them. "It's beautiful. Where do you think is the best place to plant it?" She completely ignored Monah and Casey, focusing on Luke and the plant. "Full sunlight or shade?"

Luke was in his element. Monah couldn't help but grin as she trailed behind him and Robin. They wandered for several minutes before Luke settled on the right spot. He set the plant down then stepped back.

"Mrs. Beck, did you know that purple flower is poisonous?"

CHAPTER ⛩ TWENTY-TWO

Purple flowers?

Monah advanced to Luke's side while keeping her gaze firmly fixed on Robin's face. "Where?"

Luke squatted next to them and pointed. "Right there. They're poisonous from root to stem. Even the leaves and blooms can make you very sick or kill you."

Robin's face paled. "That bad? Then why would the garden club send them to the members? Wouldn't they know that?" She turned to Lauren. "Did you know they were poisonous?"

Lauren's expression never changed. "It said as much on the packet, but I figured if the club sent them to you they couldn't be so bad. The letter they sent with the seeds said"—she tilted her head as if remembering—"the flowers would be a great addition to any garden but to wear gloves while working with them."

Brushing his hands on his pants, Luke stood. "That's because they can be highly toxic. They may be beautiful, ladies, but if I were you, I'd get rid of them. You can never be too careful."

"Would you do it for us?" Robin eyed the flowers. "You've got me terrified."

"Sure. If I can borrow a shovel, I'll put them in Monah's car and destroy them at my nursery."

Monah's mouth dropped open. "Oh no you're not. You can't put those in my car." What was he thinking? Not only didn't she want poisonous plants anywhere near her, but she couldn't risk them being seen as evidence. She'd been all through that already.

Luke smiled and shrugged. "All right, how about you also get me a trash bag, Mrs. Beck? I'll bundle it up and toss it for you. Trash day is tomorrow anyway." He turned to Monah. "That better?"

"Perfect." She moved to Casey's side. "When we finish, we need to get going. We have another stop to make." She'd seen all she wanted to at the Beck residence. Now her burning questions would be aimed at one Miss Simone Wallace.

After dropping Luke at his nursery, Monah and Casey headed to the high school. Monah finally blurted out what had been on her mind. "Can you believe that so many people could be suspects just because the garden club issued all those packets of monkshood? Why send something so poisonous? Just think of how many people they could have killed."

Casey shook her head. "Unless creating a long suspect list was just what someone on the garden-club board intended all along."

Monah gaped at Casey then had to jerk the steering wheel to keep from going off the road. "Oh my goodness. Or worse, maybe one of the club members has used this opportunity to get their dirty work done. Talk about being irresponsible." She pounded her hand on the wheel. "We need a list of the board and all club members." But would they be able to talk Simone into handing over that information?

The tune from *Magnum, P.I.* sounded from Monah's purse, and she smiled as she reached for her cell phone. "Hi, Mike." Boy, did she have some things to tell him.

"Hey, Monah. Do you have some time? I need to talk to you a few minutes."

Dread trickled through her. Why did she get the feeling this wasn't good? "Ah, actually, I'm on my way to the high school. Casey and I found out some interesting things about the garden club. I think you'd find them just as curious as we did."

Silence. What was he thinking?

"I'll meet you there."

The phone went dead before she could say a word. He wasn't his usual sweet-talking self. This was the business side of him. The side she didn't like. . .when he turned it on her. Now what happened?

Casey leaned forward. "What'd Mike say to put that frown on your face?"

"It's what he didn't say."

"Meaning?"

Monah shook her head. "It was his tone. He wants to talk to me. He's gonna meet us at the school." She pulled into the parking lot and stopped in the space nearest the front door. "Maybe it's just nerves left over from yesterday, but I get the feeling he suspects me again."

Casey unbuckled her seat belt and opened the door. "You're right. It's just nerves. But just in case, let's get in there and give him some other suspects to pursue."

The sound of their flip-flops slapping against their heels echoed down the empty hall. To Monah, the sound reminded her of those scary movies where a clock ticked off the minutes, getting louder as the time drew near for the bad guy to make his final and most deadly move.

Good grief, Monah. Get a grip.

She led the way into the office and stopped in front of Simone's desk. The secretary took her time looking up, then stared at Monah before recognition dawned on her face.

"Oh, I remember you. I wondered when you and your detective friend would be back."

Monah wanted to roll her eyes. She just bet Simone wondered when she could get her manicured claws back into Mike. The woman nearly drooled over him the last time. She felt her own nails emerging.

She forced a smile. "Hello, Miss Wallace. I've been hearing great things about your garden club and hoped you could tell me a little more about it."

Pleasure erupted on Simone's face. She leaned over her desk and laced her claws. "Really? Who have you been talking to?"

Monah didn't expect that question. "My mom's neighbors, Mr. and Mrs. Sparks."

"Oh, aren't they a sweet couple? I just love them."

Simone seemed to love everyone. Or at least the men in the world. Monah put a halt to her thoughts. She had work to do. "Do you think you could give me a list of your board and the club's members? I'd like to talk to a few more before I decide whether or not to join."

Simone tilted her head. "Why don't you just ask me your questions?"

Monah bumped her glasses higher onto her nose. "Okay, great. First, how do you and the rest of the board go about deciding which seeds to send the members?"

Simone eyed Casey. "Aren't you the girlfriend of that nursery owner?" When Casey nodded, Simone frowned. "Then why would the two of you need to join the club?"

Just answer the question! "If Luke were to give us all the plants we wanted, the poor guy would go broke. He's great for Casey, but what about me?" That's right, keep it light. No use stirring up suspicions.

"I see." Simone leaned back in her chair. "Well, we attend a conference each year. They give us great ideas. We also do a lot of our own research and talk to other clubs." She reached for one of her drawers and pulled out a catalog. "We go through several of these. Then at the meetings, we toss out ideas and narrow them down to which seeds we'll give the members and compile a list of plants we advocate as a good buy. They can place their orders through us."

"So part of the benefit of being a member is the free seeds as well as well-researched recommendations. That sounds great." Monah's mind buzzed. "Would you give me a list of the other members so I know who all I can visit who's associated with the club?"

"You're ready to become a part of our group?"

"I'm not sure yet. Is there a large cost involved? And just how many members do you already have?"

Simone pulled a folder from the same drawer as the catalog and flipped open the cover. "Here's a list. To date, we have forty-eight."

"Really? That's a lot more than I'd figured." Good grief, they'd have their work cut out for them.

"If you'd like, I can print off an application. You can take it home, look it over, and bring it back filled out if you decide to join."

This was working out perfectly. "Could you print off a list of members while you're at it?"

Simone stared at her for a moment. "I'm not sure I'm comfortable with that until you actually join."

Rats! She needed that list.

Casey leaned against the desk. "Isn't my aunt a member of your group?"

Simone crossed her arms. "And you are?"

"Casey Alexander."

"Lydia Alexander's niece? Sure. Lydia's been a member for years. Another member I love. You could ask her how she likes the club." She pursed her lips before turning to Monah. "You know, I'm surprised you haven't talked to your co-worker. She's been a member for several years."

Monah's throat dried. "My co-worker?"

"Yes." Suddenly, Simone stood, a smile stretching across her makeup-laden face. "Detective Brockman. How good to see you again." She stepped out from behind her desk and sauntered to Mike's side. "Miss Trenary never said a word about you joining us today."

Monah glared as the wench fastened herself to Mike's side. Why did he have to show up so soon? She only needed a few more minutes.

Mike briefly met her gaze then looked down at Simone. "She didn't, did she? Well, trust me, I got here as fast as I could."

As Simone beamed, Monah's hackles rose. Surely Mike wouldn't be daft enough to flirt with this woman.

Simone patted his arm then headed back to her chair. "You took your sweet time getting back here for this information. I've been saving it for you." Her eyes never once left Mike, successfully leaving Monah out of the conversation. "I thought you'd be much more interested in the infamous feud. Especially you, Miss Trenary."

Mike and Monah exchanged a glance. "What feud?" they chimed together.

Simone looked up from the papers she'd pulled from her

middle drawer and raised her brows. "What feud?" A smile crept across her face. "You haven't heard about the catfight between Miss Charlotte Tait and Sandy Magrew?"

CHAPTER ⛏⛏ ⛏⛏⛏ TWENTY-THREE

A catfight!

Mike pictured the jovial lines of Sandy's plump face, the softly curling hair, and the kind eyes. Did he really think her a murderer? It's possible, he decided. No one else had more opportunity to plant evidence that would make Monah look guilty.

"What exactly happened?" he asked, brows bunching.

"Well," Simone purred, stroking the top sheet of paper with her index finger, "it was all very long ago. Twenty years or more, if I remember right."

She twisted the large diamond ring on her finger.

"And?" Monah's voice sharpened. "So what happened?"

Without a doubt, Simone was enjoying the moment, and she refused to be prodded. "Can I get any of you something to drink?" She half rose from her chair.

"No!" Mike and Monah shouted in unison.

"Please continue," Mike said more quietly. "We're fine."

Simone smiled and resumed her seat. "It all started when a new guy, Elliot Newton, moved to Pine Mills to teach chemistry. He was handsome in his own way, what with his tweed sport coats and matching bow ties. All the ladies were infatuated, Charlotte Tait and Sandy Magrew included. Problem was, he was a confirmed bachelor and proud of it."

Mike could already see the conflict developing. "Do you have a picture of him?"

"I do." Simone rose and went to the bookshelf. Her fingers skimmed the yearbooks, finally settling on one. She took it out and flipped through the pages. "Here he is." Returning with the book, she turned it toward Mike and Monah. "Third one from the end."

Casey pushed forward to see the photo, pressing against Mike's shoulder for a better view. He readjusted his stance so she could see clearly.

Tall, thin, with a slender mustache and piercing eyes, Elliot Newton could only be described as moderately handsome, but Mike could see how someone like Charlotte Tait, single and in her early forties at the time, would be attracted to him.

He waited until Monah and Casey leaned back before pushing the yearbook to Simone. "I take it there was a battle over him?"

"More than a battle. It became competition to see which of them would finally get him to renounce his single ways. For a while, I thought it would be Charlotte, untiiillll. . ." Her voice trailed off, and she licked her lips like a cat anticipating a canary. "Sandy did the unthinkable."

"What did she do?" Monah and Casey chorused together.

Simone leaned forward, and drawn by the intensity in her stare, Mike and Monah did the same. "She ran off with him. Word around town was they had a secret rendezvous down by the beach. Boston, maybe, or Quincy Bay."

"But Sandy never married, did she?" Mike glanced at Monah then Simone. "So what happened?"

"No, she never married. Elliot Newton turned out to be a cad and moved on the moment they returned to town. Sandy was heartbroken, but Charlotte didn't care. She was furious with Sandy for stabbing her in the back. She accused her of using her youth to steal Elliot out from under her."

Mike frowned. "Her youth?"

Monah nodded. "She's at least ten years younger than Miss Tait."

"Oh."

"Which is why Miss Tait had so much pull with the board when the time came to hire a new library aide at the high school." Simone waited, fingers drumming.

"You mean?" Monah's mouth dropped.

"Exactly. Sandy applied. When Miss Tait heard they were considering her for the position, she went to the board and voiced 'her concerns.' Charlotte had connections, even back then—two brothers in circuit court, an uncle at the police department. The board was afraid to cross her, so they hired someone else, and Sandy was furious."

Mike nodded. "I really appreciate your help, Simone. We won't take up too much more of your time, but I do have just a couple more questions."

She shrugged. "Not a problem."

"There's no doubt this is all very interesting, but do you have anything to support what you've just shared with us?"

Peeking over her shoulder, she pulled the papers out from under the folder and slid them to him. "These minutes show everyone who addressed the board that night. My private notes." She tapped the page underneath. "Fill in the details."

"You were there?" Monah's brow rose.

Simone's lips hardened. "I was very young when I hired on."

The sparks passing between the two women were tangible. Time to head off the turn in the conversation. "One last thing,"

Mike said, tucking the notes under his arm. "What can you tell me about Greg Dyer?"

Startled for a moment, Simone blinked. "Mr. Dyer?"

"Didn't I see him coming inside the same day Monah and I first spoke to you?"

Gradually, the confusion cleared from her face. "Oh yes. I remember now. He asked for the board minutes from the past several months."

Mike chewed the information. "Would it be possible to get copies of everything you gave him? Whatever you can remember?" He hesitated and shot Monah a sidewise glance. She wasn't going to like this. He cleared his throat, leaned toward Simone, and lowered his voice. "I'd, um, really appreciate it."

The smile and wink that followed worked magic on the secretary. She beamed at him then turned to the computer and pulled up the file. Within moments, he had the papers in his hand.

Well, he'd gotten what he'd come for, though at a price. As they left the school, Mike did his best to ignore the steam coming from Monah.

~

Monah wanted to stomp her feet and beat Mike's chest. How could he flirt like that again? And right in front of her! Just wait until she got him alone. Until then. . .

Why didn't Sandy tell her about what had happened with Miss Tait? The story sure explained why she acted so uncomfortable about Veronica's feud comment made at the city council meeting. Unease trembled through Monah. There were only two reasons Sandy kept quiet. Either she didn't want to face suspicion—and Monah understood that completely—or she was guilty. The last thought made her heart clench. Not

Sandy. She couldn't kill someone. The worst she did was spread gossip about the sins of others.

Once outside, Mike moved to her side. "I need to talk to Sandy."

Monah picked up her pace, but Mike's long strides caught him up in a hurry. Still displeased with him, she couldn't bring herself to be of much help. "Why the need to talk to her? You know she's not any guiltier than I am."

"Don't be difficult, Monah. You heard the same thing I did. Sandy just moved to the number one spot on my suspect list."

"Right above me, you mean?"

Mike grabbed her arm and spun her around. "I apologized for that. And now I apologize for the way I coaxed Miss Wallace into giving me these papers."

"Coaxed? Is that what men call flirting these days?"

At least he had the decency to look ashamed.

"Granted there was probably a better way to go about it." He took her into his arms and looked deeply into her eyes. "I'm sorry for taking the easy way. I promise I won't do it again."

Why did he have to look so handsome. . .and sincere? And why didn't he realize she wanted him to seal the promise with a kiss? Her anger fizzled like a wet match. She poked him in the chest. "I'm gonna hold you to that."

He grabbed her finger and pressed it to his lips. "You can hold me all you want."

Doggone it. He got himself out of that way too easily, but she sure liked the way he went about it. She softened like warm butter. "You sure you have to talk to Sandy?"

He continued to hold her. "She's one of the few allowed behind the counter, which is where I found the monkshood seeds. She had access to all those gardening books."

A cold sweat broke out down Monah's back as all the evidence piled on top of what she'd learned from Simone. She had to tell him. "That's not all, Mike."

She pulled away from him so she could think clearly. She waved Casey over when she saw her by the car. Casey must have distanced herself to give them some privacy. What a great friend. But now Monah needed her support.

Mike must have waited all he could stand. "Well?" He looked from one to the other. "What else is there?"

Oh, but she didn't want to tell this. "Yesterday, at my mom's, I heard the neighbors arguing in their garden. I went out there when I saw Mrs. Sparks holding purple flowers." She took a deep breath. "It was monkshood."

Mike frowned. "Are you telling me you think they did it?"

"No." Why was this so hard? "I asked them about it, and they said the garden club they belonged to sent it to them. When Casey and I went to Robin Beck's house earlier, she had the same thing in her garden. She also belongs to the garden club."

Mike examined her face as he processed the information. She could see the moment it all registered. "So everyone in the garden club is a suspect."

"Or one of the people on the board who decided to send the poisonous seeds to all forty-eight members."

The tiniest of smiles curled the corners of Mike's mouth. "Don't tell me. You already found out who all is on the board."

Monah licked her lips. "I know one. Simone Wallace."

Mike cranked his head around toward the school. He turned back more slowly. Monah could almost see the thoughts dashing through his mind. Hers were also on the move. Mike paced in front of them. His hand moved to the back of his neck while the other propped on his hip. Then he stopped and faced them.

"Okay, help me think this through. Miss Tait and Wayne Drolen both die from monkshood poisoning. Everyone in the garden club has monkshood growing in their gardens. Simone Wallace is on the board of that club and just pointed us toward suspecting Sandy Magrew as the killer. Yet Simone works at the same school as Miss Tait and had access to her and monkshood. Is that everything?"

Casey scratched her forehead. "Not exactly."

Mike speared them both with a stern gaze. "What else?"

Monah rubbed at her arms, suddenly feeling chilled though standing in full sunlight. "Sandy is a member of the garden club."

As the news sank in, Mike's shoulders slumped. He lifted one finger. "Sandy works at the library where Miss Tait died." He lifted two more fingers. "She has access to both the water bottles and monkshood." Another finger rose. "Wayne died after drinking from one of those bottles." Mike showed all five members of his hand. "She belongs to the garden club. That's quite a handful of evidence, ladies. Do I dare ask if there's anything else?"

Feeling completely sick to her stomach, Monah nodded. "She's the one who purchased the bottles of water for the fund-raiser."

Mike placed his hands on her shoulders. "I'm going to have to question her, Monah." He lifted her chin when she didn't look at him. "And when I finish with her, I'll have to question Miss Wallace."

Monah's mouth dropped open to protest. He put his finger to her lips.

"Strictly business. I promise."

This time, he sealed it with a kiss.

CHAPTER TWENTY-FOUR

The scent of Monah's perfume intoxicated Mike's senses and filled him with warmth. He drew back, his head spinning. "Wow."

"Yeah, wow." A lazy smile crept across Monah's lips.

Resisting the urge to claim them again, Mike lifted his finger and gently stroked her cheek. "I could get used to that."

"I could let you."

He returned her smile. Maybe he would kiss her again, just to prove the effect of the last one hadn't been a fluke. He leaned closer.

"Um, excuse me."

Both he and Monah swiveled to look at Casey. He'd forgotten she was even there.

She lifted her hands, palms up. "I hate to interrupt, but if we're going to question Sandy—"

"Whoa." He straightened up. "There's no 'we.' I'll be conducting the interview with Sandy by myself."

"But, Mike—"

"No 'buts,' " he said, holding up his hand to stop Monah's protest. "This isn't an official interrogation, but I still think it would be better if I handled it myself."

She folded her arms, all traces of affection wiped clean off her face. "I see."

"Monah. . ." He could make ice with the sudden chill that had taken over the air.

"So you're going to haul her to the station—is that it?"

"No—"

"Treat Sandy like a common criminal?"

"Of course not. I just intend to ask her a few questions."

"Right. And then what? I suppose you plan to pull into her driveway with your siren blaring. I'm sure her neighbors won't have a thing to say." She stomped her foot. "Do you even know how many tongues will wag?"

Mike hesitated. She had a point. The neighbors would wonder why he was there, even if he didn't pull up with the siren blaring. Presuming she was innocent, he really didn't want to do that to her. "I could talk to her at the library, I suppose. She might be more comfortable there than she would be at the station."

Monah lifted a brow. "Really? And how will you do that? The library's closed."

He scratched his head. She sure wasn't making this easy.

"Ah, can I offer a suggestion?"

He gratefully swung his gaze to Casey. "Absolutely."

Casey tapped her temple, thinking. "Okay Mike, you could interview Sandy at the library. Monah, you could let him in, right?"

She scowled. "I suppose, but she won't come. She watches that dance show on Thursday nights."

"She would if you called and told her you needed her help with something."

Monah shook her head violently. "No way. I'm not luring her down there so Mike can interrogate her."

Not fair. He had no intention of interrogating Sandy,

and Monah knew it.

"Hear me out." Casey turned to look at Mike, her blue eyes wide and innocent. "Monah will help you get Sandy to the library. In return, you let Monah be present when you question her."

"What?" Mike's mouth fell. "Wait just a minute—"

"Sounds fair to me." A satisfied smirk curled Monah's lips. "I'll do it."

"Hold up, I never agreed—"

"You have Sandy's number?" Casey asked.

Holding up her phone, Monah nodded. "Right here." She quirked an eyebrow at Mike. "Well?"

He glanced at the two. *Women!* They could be downright impossible. Still, all he had against Sandy was hearsay at the moment, and until he got some concrete evidence, the most he could do was ask some general questions. There really wasn't anything to stop Monah from sitting in as long as Sandy agreed. "Fine. But if at any point this becomes more than just an informal inquiry, I'll have to take her in."

"Agreed." Monah hit SEND on her phone then put it to her ear. After a brief pause, she said, "Hello, Sandy? It's Monah." She listened for a moment. "No, everything's fine, but I wonder if you would come down to the library for a bit." Her gaze, slightly troubled, locked with Mike's. "There's something I need your help with." She nodded to something Sandy said. "Yes, I know it's Thursday night, but this really is quite important. I wouldn't ask otherwise." Another pause. "No, I'd really rather not say until you get to the library. I'm sorry, Sandy. I know that's a lot to ask."

Monah's eyes misted. "Thanks, Sandy. I'll meet you there." She closed the phone. "She's on her way."

A twinge of guilt fired in Mike's gut. Monah was a dyed-in-the-wool, lay-down-your-life-for-a-friend type of gal. Too bad he couldn't have done this without involving her. He squeezed her hand. "Thanks."

She shook her head. "Don't thank me. I feel terrible."

Casey slipped her arm around Monah's shoulders. "Don't worry. All of this will be cleared up as soon as Mike is finished asking his questions."

He hoped so. Deep down, he wasn't so sure, but that wasn't what Monah needed to hear. "You're probably right."

Monah sniffed then nodded.

Mike led them to Monah's car and tucked them inside. "I'll meet you at the library," he said, tapping the roof.

A few minutes later, they were pulling up to the library parking lot. Sandy was already there.

"What's this all about?" she said, looking from Mike to Monah to Casey. She was wearing a jogging suit, and her hair was done up in curlers. No doubt she'd planned on spending a quiet evening at home. Hopefully, she still would.

Mike gestured toward the library. "I've got a few simple questions for you, Sandy. I figured it would be best to ask them here rather than at the station."

Sandy's face paled, and she pressed her hand to her ample chest. "The station? Why? Have I done something wrong?"

"No, ma'am, it's not that. I just need a few answers that only you can supply. If you don't mind, Monah would like to sit in. She thought it might make you feel a little more comfortable."

Sandy's lip trembled. "Monah?"

"It'll be fine," Monah assured, moving to wrap Sandy in a hug. "He really does have just a few simple questions. You don't mind, do you?"

Her expression still troubled, Sandy shrugged. "I guess not."

"Let's go inside then, shall we?" Mike extended his hand to

the door and then followed the women up the steps. Once inside, he selected a table and pulled out two chairs, one for Monah and one for Sandy.

Casey excused herself. "I'll just wait over there." She pointed to a section displaying several Brandy Purcell mysteries.

Mike nodded. Once everyone was situated, he got down to business. "I understand you were the one who purchased the water bottles the day Wayne Drolen died."

Sandy's head bobbed. "That's right. We were running low, so Monah sent me to the store for more."

Withdrawing a notepad and pen from his shirt pocket, Mike flipped open to a blank page. "Mind telling me where you bought it?"

"Finch's Grocery. They had it on sale, so I picked up several cases." She glanced at Monah nervously. "Monah said it was okay."

"Good." Mike wrote the information in his notebook. "Were you also the one who stored the water in the cooler?"

"Uh-huh." She swallowed hard, her hands twisting in her lap. "Is that important?"

"Just making sure I cover everything," Mike said.

Monah patted her arm. "You're doing fine."

"Thanks."

"Sandy, do you remember noticing if any of the seals on the bottles were broken?"

She shook her head. "I really didn't look that close."

He hadn't expected her to remember. "Okay. What about the day Charlotte Tait was killed? Anything more you can remember about that day?"

Sandy rubbed her chin. "Nothing."

He hesitated and shifted so that he could clearly see Sandy's face and body language. The way she reacted to his next question would tell him a lot. "Sandy, is it true that you and Charlotte Tait had a history of animosity over a man who once taught in Pine Mills?"

Sandy blanched. She stared at Monah. "Is that what this is about?"

Monah's face fell into a grimace. "I'm sorry, Sandy. We went by the superintendent's office today looking for evidence. Simone Wallace told us about the bad blood between you two."

Sadness flooded Sandy's features, and her plump shoulders drooped. "It's been so many years. I figured all of that had finally been laid to rest." She drew a deep breath and looked Mike square in the eye. "It's true that Charlotte and I squabbled. Elliot was a dream come true, or so we both thought. Turned out he was a scoundrel." Remorse replaced the sudden spark of defiance. "That still doesn't excuse what I did."

Mike laid his pen on the table. "What was that?"

Her cheeks flushed red. "I thought I could steal him away from Charlotte if I agreed. . .he asked. . ." She paused and colored deeper. "We went away for the weekend. I'm not proud of it. Charlotte was shocked and hurt when we got back to town, and I don't blame her. I still never expected her to go to the school board the way she did. They turned me down for a job. I admit, I was mad at the time, but that was eons ago. I would never dream of bringing harm to her over it now. Besides, if I'd wanted to hurt her over something so trivial, why would I have waited years to do it?"

She had a point. He flipped to another page. "One last thing. You belong to the garden club here in town, right?"

Sandy nodded. "That's right."

"Can you tell me how long you've been a member?"

She looked up and to the left. "Gosh, I don't know. . . three or four years, maybe."

He jotted the information down. "Monah says this last shipment of plants you received contained monkshood seeds. Were you aware of that?"

Sandy blushed and shook her head. "Actually, no. I've been so busy this summer I haven't bothered to look. The box is still in my garage, unopened."

Monah's eyes widened, and a smile burst onto her lips. "Really?"

"Really." Sandy looked at Mike. "Why do you ask?"

"Just trying to narrow down the people with possible access to the seeds. You wouldn't mind if I took a look at that box, would you?"

"I don't mind a bit. You can come now if you like."

The look Monah directed at him was positively triumphant. She hugged Sandy's shoulders. "Thanks so much for agreeing to these questions."

Sandy glanced at Mike. "Is that it?"

He nodded. "For now. I may have more questions later. Will that be okay?"

"Fine."

With each word, Monah appeared more and more pleased. It was obvious that in her mind Sandy had already proved her innocence. Mike wasn't so sure. The problem was, unless he came up with some solid evidence, *he* had no way of proving it.

CHAPTER TWENTY-FIVE

Monah twisted the lock on the library doors and blew a weary sigh. What a day. To be bombarded by so much information and still be no closer to knowing the killer's identity was not the way she wanted it to end. Worse yet, she had the feeling Sandy no longer trusted her or, at the very least, held doubts about the strength of their friendship.

With a shake of her head, she made her way to the table where Casey waited for her. "Thanks for staying a little longer. I have some thoughts I need to bounce off someone."

Casey leaned forward. "You don't think we've got the real murderer on your list, do you?"

Stunned, Monah's heart thumped. "How did you know that?"

"I feel the same way. We have a whole list of suspects, yet none of them feel right, like they could actually plan a murder and carry it out, let alone two."

Excitement charged to Monah's nerve endings. "Right. So have you come up with any other answers?"

Casey laughed. "No. With everything going on, I couldn't concentrate." She pulled out a pad of Post-it notes and a pen from her purse. "But we can start by putting our heads together."

"Great." Monah rubbed her hands together. "Okay, we thought Robin or Lauren could have done it, but as far as I know, they only had access to Miss Tait."

"And they seem the least likely to kill someone. They were genuinely shocked to find out they had a poisonous plant in their garden." Casey scratched through the Beck names. "What about the teens we have listed? We've already crossed off most of them."

Monah folded her arms on the table. "As far as I'm concerned, you can cross off all of them. They only wanted Miss Tait out of the picture. None of them had any dealings with Wayne."

Casey flicked her pen between her thumb and finger. "What about the crafty secretary Simone Wallace?"

"What about her?" Monah's claws emerged. The idea of Mike going back there with more questions made her grit her teeth so she wouldn't scream.

"Hey." Casey smiled. "Mike's not interested in her. Besides, he promised not to flirt."

Monah wanted to fuss and fume and demand he not return, but if she were honest, it was her own insecurities she fought. Self-esteem was her ongoing battle, and now was the time to face it head-on.

Casey grasped her hand. "Mike only has eyes for you."

Warmth bubbled through her. "Yeah, he really does, doesn't he?" Heart lifted, she forced her mind back to the problem at hand. "Simone had access to Miss Tait but not Wayne. Seems like most everyone had a chance or reason to go after Miss Tait but not Wayne. I think that's what we need to focus on." She tapped the table with her finger. "Who had a reason to want Wayne dead?"

"Don't get mad, but what about Sandy? I think we need to make this clear. We both agree that she's an unlikely suspect even though she had access to both Miss Tait and Wayne as well as the water bottles, right?"

Monah shuddered. "It sounds bad when you put it that way. But honestly, I don't think she's capable of murder. Hatred and desperation are two of the biggest motives for killing someone. Neither one of those is in her."

"Agreed. All right, let's look at this list again but only at the ones who could have gotten to Wayne at the fund-raiser."

Monah silently read through the remaining names on the list. Jimmy Capps. She hadn't even seen him at the fund-raiser. Greg Dyer. Hmm. Not only did he have a problem with Miss Tait, but he could have run into trouble with Wayne since he was the real estate agent for Wayne's property. And what about those pieces of paper they found in the warehouse that was supposed to be vacant? She was about to say as much when Casey spun her Post-it pad around with only one name.

"Ken Greer?"

Casey tapped the tip of her pen next to the name. "Think about it. First, he had access to both Miss Tait and Wayne Drolen. He was at the library the day Miss Tait died, and he had one of the main attractions at the fund-raiser." She pulled the pad back and wrote more below the name. "And second, there's a connection between him and the two victims."

Monah read the words upside down. A chill ran down her spine. "Donated funds." She swallowed hard. "They all wanted them."

"Exactly. And so do you and Mike."

Monah lifted her gaze to meet Casey's. "But we're innocent."

"Without a doubt. Which leaves only one other person who wants the funds and might be eliminating the competition."

"Ken Greer."

"Exactly," Casey said. "I think we should follow him around

for a while, see what he's up to."

"Why?"

Casey again grasped Monah's hand. "There's still two more in the competition he needs to remove."

Monah's mouth went dry. She couldn't put voice to the words, but they thrummed through her mind like an unending drumbeat. *Mike and me.*

~

Tick, tick, tick.

The clock above Mike's head tracked the passing seconds without mercy, and with no activity buzzing through the station at this late hour, it was abnormally loud. Or maybe it was his nerves that made it seem so. After all, he'd been sitting at his desk since he left Sandy's house. Her box from the garden club had indeed appeared unopened, and there had been no tampering evident on the seal.

Arms in front of him, he laced his fingers and stretched until his knuckles cracked. It brought little relief. He was tired, hungry, and more than a little cranky that despite the time he'd put in on this case, he had nothing solid.

Returning his attention to the case, he sifted through his notes. Something about the conversation with Sandy didn't sit right. He should be more convinced that she killed Charlotte Tait. She had opportunity. She had motive. But what about Wayne Drolen? What possible connection did she have with him?

Mentally, he ticked off the information he knew about Drolen. He was a councilman with the city. He wanted and pushed for the new sports complex. Several of his properties were involved in the arsons around town. Greg Dyer was his real estate agent.

Greg Dyer.

Mike smacked his head and riffled quickly through his case

file. Days ago, he'd seen Greg Dyer in the Drolen home. That meant the Drolens and Dyers had been close. Dyer was on the school board, something Charlotte Tait would obviously take an interest in. Plus, Monah said something about seeing him pass money to Miss Tait. It was a shaky connection at best, but at least it was something.

His fingers settled on the school board minutes Simone Wallace said Dyer had requested. He skimmed the first page. Resignation letters. Bid notices on classroom equipment. Nothing unusual except for a note about Dyer recommending the use of Atlantic Paper districtwide.

He flipped to the next page. Again, Dyer recommending Atlantic Paper. This time, a comparison cost sheet listing several other paper companies was attached. Atlantic Paper wasn't the lowest bid, so why had Dyer been compelled to push for it?

A tiny alarm bell went off in his head. Where had he seen the name *Atlantic Paper* before? Pressing his fingers to his forehead, he closed his eyes to think.

Aargh!

When nothing came, Mike shoved to his feet and walked to the coffeepot to pour another cup. The caffeine would keep him up, but what difference did it make? He doubted he'd sleep much until he figured this case out anyway.

The scalding liquid was bitter on his tongue. Lois had made it before she left, so it had sat on the burner for over two hours. Bernice, the night dispatcher, didn't drink coffee.

Bingham's warehouse.

The answer struck him suddenly. He set down his cup with a *thud*, sloshing hot liquid over the side. Muttering to himself, Mike shook the scalding coffee off his hand. He'd seen something about Atlantic Paper in the arson report Ken gave him. Wiping the remaining spilled coffee from his fingers onto his jeans, he crossed to the filing cabinet, jerked out the report, and carried it to his desk. Sure enough. Ken listed a box from Atlantic Paper as part of the accelerant used to start the Bingham warehouse fire and included a scrap from the label as evidence.

Suspicion crept into Mike's mind. Dyer was involved in something underhanded, if not illegal. He was certain of it. Perhaps that involvement had led to the fires.

Now the question was, what connection did Dyer have to the murders?

CHAPTER ⚡⚡⚡ TWENTY-SIX

Monah flipped her cell phone closed, ending her conversation with Sandy. The poor thing didn't sound too happy. She probably didn't get much sleep last night after being questioned by Mike, and now Monah told her she'd be late for work. . .again. Sandy would be in charge of the library and the summer help. . .again. Monah couldn't fault her for being grouchy.

She didn't get a full night's rest either. The idea of Ken killing off the competition for the donated funds filled her with enough unease to make her want to sleep with one eye and both ears open. Yet the image of Greg Dyer sitting with Miss Tait at the library table on the day she died continued to surface.

The driveway in front of Lydia Alexander's house sloped gently between two rows of crape myrtles. What rotten timing for Lydia's car to break down. Casey was sweet to offer her aunt Lydia the use of hers, but Monah lost valuable minutes picking Casey up. Ken could be anywhere by the time she and Casey made it back to town. How were they supposed to tail him if they couldn't find him?

Pasting a smile on her face to cover her grump, Monah headed toward the porch. Lydia and Casey appeared in the doorway. Casey held a travel mug that was sure to be full of coffee. Why didn't Monah think of that? She'd need all the help she could get today. Maybe. . .

She pointed at the mug. "Do you have an extra one of those?"

Lydia beamed. "Absolutely. Come on in."

Monah trailed after her, but when they reached the kitchen, her eyes zeroed in on the pan of brownies sitting on the table rather than the coffeepot.

"Help yourself, Monah." Lydia wasn't even looking at her but still knew her well enough to know she'd like a brownie. . .or two.

Grinning, Casey slid the pan toward her. "You wanna just take the whole thing?"

Monah made a face as she picked up a spatula, held it in her fist, and pointed it at Casey. "Yes, but I won't."

Chocolate was her downfall. If someone could figure out how to make a chocolate pot roast, she'd buy shares. Instead she scooped a large portion of the brownies out and put them on a paper towel, then reached for the coffee Lydia handed her. "Thank you, Lydia. At least *someone* around here looks out for me."

Lydia laughed as she followed them to the door. "You two be careful today."

"We will," they chimed.

"Uh-huh." Lydia climbed into Casey's silver BMW and drove off down the driveway.

Her hands full, Monah stood next to her car staring at the door.

Huffing good-naturedly, Casey made her way around the front. "Need some help?"

Monah narrowed her eyes. "Don't make me hurt you."

Casey laughed and opened the door, then circled back to the passenger side and climbed in. Monah settled her coffee and took a big bite of a brownie before starting the car. "Mmm." She closed her eyes while savoring the taste.

"Hello. You act like you haven't eaten in a week."

"Yeah, but I haven't had a brownie in at least a month." She chomped off another piece before backing out to the road. "You think we should start at the station first? It's getting kinda late. I don't know where Ken will be."

"Sounds like a plan. You want me to drive so you can finish that without getting us in a wreck?"

"Oh, ha-ha." She set the remainder of the brownies on the console then broke off a piece and shoved it in her mouth before gripping the steering wheel. "Look, Mom, both hands."

As they zipped down the road, Monah silently thanked the Lord again for Casey's friendship. From the start, they got along as though they'd always known each other. And now, she had a sleuthing buddy, one who loved the Brandy Purcell books, which led her back to her earlier thought.

"Hey, Case, I realize we both think Ken is the best suspect, but I can't get rid of a bad feeling about Greg Dyer."

"Why's that? Because you saw him with Miss Tait?"

The image played through Monah's mind again. "Yeah, I guess. But he also has a connection to Wayne. A big one." She thought it through again. "He had a chance to poison Miss Tait right there at the library table, but how did he manage to poison Wayne? You think Greg gave Wayne some water after I did?"

"Possible. Almost everyone knew what kind of water you were giving away. What better way to pin the murder on you than to use the same brand?"

A blast of anger rocketed through Monah. "And Ken could have done the same thing. It's no secret what kind I always get."

"Hey, hold up." Casey leaned forward to stare out the windshield. "Slow down."

"What's wrong?"

Casey pointed. "Isn't that Ken's pickup?"

The hunter green truck bounced from a side road onto the highway. In moments the distance between it and Monah widened. She accelerated to catch up.

"Wait." Casey thumped the dash. "What are you doing? Turn into the drive he came from."

Monah slowed. "Why? I thought we were gonna follow him."

"So we can see what's back there. See what he's been up to."

Monah pulled to a stop at the entrance to the dirt lane. Or maybe she should say "mud lane." "I'm not going down there."

"Don't be silly. Turn in."

"Are you going to push me out when I get stuck?"

Casey scowled. "You're not gonna get stuck. Let's go."

"I'm not going. He has a four-wheel drive pickup. My car won't make it ten feet."

Casey stared out the side window then opened the door. Monah grabbed her arm.

"Where do you think you're going?"

"We'll walk."

"Get back in here." She waited for Casey to close the door. "I'll tell you what's down there. An abandoned cabin and boathouse. Both are nearly falling to the ground. There. Now there's no need for either of us to go."

"A lake is back there? Cool."

Monah rolled her eyes. "We need to get going so we can catch up to Ken and see where he's headed."

"But—"

"No." Monah stomped on the gas pedal.

They rode in near silence the remainder of the way into town. Ken's truck was parked outside the fire station. Monah pulled to the side of the road and stopped under a tree, prepared to stay as long as necessary.

An hour and a half later, doing little more than talking about Brandy Purcell books, Casey huffed. "See? We could have scoped out the boathouse and still made it back here in time to watch Ken do nothing."

Monah grinned. "And here all I was doing was thinking I should have taken the whole pan of brownies instead of just half."

Casey peered at her over her sunglasses then burst out laughing. "Only you, Monah."

The words were barely out of her mouth when the horn came on in front of the station. The large front door rolled open, and the truck rushed out, its lights and sirens going. The truck's tires nearly squealed as Ken turned the corner.

Without a word, Monah cranked her own engine to follow. She craned her neck to look at the sky. Black smoke spiraled up before the wind caught it and dragged it sideways. She glanced at Casey. They were headed back in the direction they'd come.

CHAPTER ⛬ TWENTY-SEVEN

Dyer Realty sat nestled between a hardware store and a bakery, the smell from which set Mike's stomach rumbling. His vehicle idling, he watched as Greg unlocked the front door and flipped over the CLOSED sign.

He checked his watch. Seven thirty-five. The guy reported to work early. He waited. A few minutes later, the front door opened and Greg stepped over to the bakery. He disappeared for a moment then reemerged carrying a white paper bag.

Perfect. Mike should have almost a full half hour before anyone else showed up. Picking the items off the seat that he'd grabbed on a hunch, he climbed out of the car and followed Greg into the realty office.

"Morning, Detective," Greg said as the buzzer above the door sounded. He held up the bag. "You're just in time. Dosie's donuts are the best. Care for some coffee?" He gestured to a pot hissing through the brew cycle. "It'll be ready in a little bit."

Mike shook his head. "No thanks. I've already had a cup."

Greg's desk, larger than the receptionist's and situated further to the rear of the office, was loaded with files, photos, and keys. He cleared a space and set the bag down. "What can I do for you?"

The direct approach usually worked best. Mike relaxed his

stance and crossed his arms. "What can you tell me about Atlantic Paper?"

Greg paled and stumbled back a step. "At–Atlantic Paper?" Circling his desk, he dropped into his chair. "Nothing. Why?"

Mike shrugged and motioned to a chair. "May I?"

Greg nodded, and Mike sat.

He eyed Greg steadily. "I'm surprised. I noticed that you pushed for their bid last year when the Pine Mills School Board was looking for a new paper supplier."

"Oh, that." Greg's shoulders relaxed. "If I remember right, their quote was a little higher than a couple of the others, but the quality was better. I use it here in my office." He swiveled in his chair, removed a sheet from the printer on a table behind him, and passed it to Mike.

Mike fingered the edge. "Looks like paper to me."

"It's a brighter white. Plus, the weight is good."

Quirking a brow, Mike nodded. "I guess so." He passed the paper back. "Was that the only reason you wanted them?"

Greg laid the sheet on some folders and folded his hands on top of the stack. "Of course."

The two men eyed each other.

The coffeepot gurgled noisily, and Greg got up to pour himself a cup. Lifting the mug, he glanced at Mike. "Sure I can't get you any?"

"I'm fine."

He added two creamer packets and sweetener then carried the mug back to his desk, swirling a coffee stirrer through the liquid. "So, you interested in looking at a property?"

Mike shook his head. "Actually, I need to ask you about a property you have listed."

His composure recovered, Greg tapped the stirrer on the rim

of his cup, sucked the end, then dropped it in the trash. His chair squeaked as he resumed his seat and leaned back. "Really? Which one?"

"Bingham's warehouse."

Greg took his time answering. He sipped from his cup before setting it on an electric warmer and flicking it on.

"The warehouse, eh? Yeah, it was a real bummer seeing that one go up in smoke. I didn't realize you were interested in that kind of property."

"I'm not."

Greg looked at him steadily then sat forward. "Is this an official visit, Detective?"

Abandoning the casual stance, Mike matched his posture. "Mr. Dyer, was the warehouse used for storage of any kind?"

"I don't think so. Why?"

Taking a plastic bag from his pocket, Mike pushed it across the desk to Greg. Inside were the charred remains of the Atlantic Paper label Ken gave him. Greg looked only mildly interested.

"What's that?"

"I was hoping you could tell me."

" 'Fraid not." He took a sip from his mug then grabbed the bakery bag and removed a donut hole. Popping it into his mouth, he licked the sugar from his fingers and reached for a napkin. "Delicious. Nothing like a warm donut hole."

This was not going the way Mike had hoped. Greg seemed way too confident. He reached into his pocket and took out the last item he'd brought, but instead of sliding it to Greg, he laid it on the desk in front of him.

Greg stopped chewing and stared. Slowly, he swallowed and lifted his gaze to Mike's. "Is this a bribe?"

Finally. The guy looked rattled. He was onto something.

Mike shook his head and tapped the twenty-dollar bill. "I think you know exactly what it is."

Indecision wavered on Greg's face for a moment before crumbling into defeat. "I'm going to need my lawyer."

Mike drew a deep breath. He'd done it! He'd caught his killer. Elation surged through him. He rose to his feet. "You might get a judge to go easier on you if you tell me why you murdered Charlotte Tait and Wayne Drolen."

"What?" Greg's head shot up. "I didn't murder them. The money, yes. I admit I helped a guy out of Boston create the counterfeits. We stored it at Bingham's until he could line up a means of moving it out, but I panicked."

Confused, Mike stared at the beaten real estate agent. "You'd better fill me in on exactly what you've been up to, Mr. Dyer."

Greg let go a lengthy sigh and waved to the chair. Mike sat.

"It all started last summer. You knew I bought a boat?"

Mike nodded. "I remember hearing something."

"Well, I met a man at the marina where I keep it stored. He was younger than me but well-off, and he offered me a deal I couldn't refuse."

"Go on."

Greg blew out a breath. He jerked to his feet and went to stand by the window.

"His name is Randall Walker. He's a salesman for Atlantic Paper. He convinced me to pressure the school board into entering a deal with his company so that we could get an unlimited supply of the stock we needed to make the counterfeit bills. Afterward, all I had to do was store the money. He took care of the rest."

Mike took out his notepad and wrote down the name. "His contact? Ink and plates?"

Greg shook his head. "I didn't ask questions. My cut wasn't

that big, but it was worth it for the little I had to do."

"You said you panicked. Why?"

Turning from the window, Greg sighed. "My son, Paul, got his hands on a few of the bills. He owed Miss Tait for a book he never returned, and rather than tell us about it, he used the money to pay her. She recognized the fake bill and warned me about it at the library the day she died."

Mike glanced at the twenty on the desk. "So this wasn't money you were giving to her?"

Greg shook his head. "She was giving it back to me. Said she knew it was fake and planned on going to the police."

"Then how come she still had it?"

"We were interrupted before she could give it to me."

"Which prompted you to burn the rest so it couldn't be used as evidence."

"Exactly."

"What about the other fires?"

"I had nothing to do with them."

"And the murders?"

"Like I said, Detective, I never killed anyone."

Mike studied the worry lining Greg's face. His eyes were red, tired, but he met Mike's gaze steadily.

"Can I call my lawyer now?"

After a moment, Mike nodded. Greg was telling the truth. He sensed it, and his instincts had never led him wrong before. While that meant he'd solved at least one of the fires, it still left many questions unanswered, including the most important one—the identity of the murderer in Pine Mills.

CHAPTER TWENTY-EIGHT

Monah stomped on the gas pedal trying to keep up with the fire truck.

"Watch out!" Casey braced her hands on the dash.

A navy blue pickup darted from the left. Monah slammed on her brakes as she pulled to the right. Another truck passed from behind, its emergency light bar flashing. Monah ran her trembling hand over her cheek.

"That was close."

Casey patted her shoulder. "Yeah. Ken must have called in all the volunteers. Keep going. I'll help you watch for others."

As badly as Monah wanted to stay where it was safe, she wanted to know even more where the emergency vehicles were going. She eased back on the road. "I should call Mike."

"You drive. I'll call him. Where's your phone?"

"Inside my purse."

Monah concentrated, pulling to the side to allow another truck to zip by, while Casey talked. Casey flipped the phone closed and tossed it into the console pocket.

"His office already called him. He asked, since he knew he couldn't stop you from going, would you at least be careful?"

Monah gave a shaky laugh. "I'm trying."

The closer they drew, the larger the black smoke cloud loomed.

Casey shook her head. "I thought you said there was only an abandoned cabin and boathouse down there."

"There is."

"Well, that sure is a lot of smoke for something like that."

Monah agreed. The last time she'd been to the cabin, the wood was so rotted it shouldn't have taken but a few minutes for the place to be consumed. She stopped on the side of the road right before she reached the lane. The blue pickup that had almost hit her was stuck halfway to the tree line.

"I can't go back there, Case."

"I know. But at least we found out for sure the fire's in the same place Ken came from."

"Yeah. Sure doesn't look good for him, does it?"

They sat silent, watching, waiting for Mike to arrive. Monah finally put voice to her burning question.

"Why would Ken set fires? He's a fireman. It makes no sense."

Casey shrugged. "I was wondering the same thing. Maybe he wants to show the town how desperately we need more help."

Monah snorted. "We wouldn't need more help if he wouldn't set fires."

"I know. Sometimes there's no way to fathom the way people think."

"Ain't it the truth?" She glanced in her rearview mirror. "Mike's here."

He pulled up behind them and got out. They did the same. He took Monah by the hand and led her to the other side of the car. "You two okay?"

"Yeah." Monah glanced toward the fire. The smoke was almost gone. "Mike, there's something you need to know."

The muscles along his jaw clenched. "Do I *want* to know? You two didn't get into trouble, did you?"

She peeked at Casey. "Of course not. Have we ever?" She waved her hand. "Never mind. Just let me tell you what we learned about Ken today."

"Ken?" His brows rose. "What?"

Monah cleared her throat. "We were planning to tail him around."

Mike's face showed the question before the word was spoken. "Why?"

"He seemed to be the only connection between Wayne and Miss Tait. We were on our way back into town after picking Casey up this morning and saw Ken come out"— she turned and pointed—"from there."

Monah was pointing down the lane toward the boathouse. Disappointment and anger twisted in Mike's gut. He liked Ken. He was a good friend. He worked hard at his job and believed in what he did. Mike shoved his hands into his pockets. "How long ago was that?"

"About three hours?" Monah looked at Casey for affirmation; she nodded. "Okay."

She looked so small standing there staring up at him, and Mike still didn't know how much Ken was capable of. He took her hand and gave it a squeeze. "Will you do me a favor? Take Casey and go back to the library." She opened her mouth and tried to tug her hand away, but Mike quickly placed his finger over her lips. "I'll tell you everything when I get there. I promise."

"But, Mike—"

Heart thumping, he grasped her and pulled her to his chest. Didn't she know how important she was to him? If anything happened to her—

"Please," he whispered against her hair. "I've got a hunch you're right about Ken, and there's too much to do for me to be worried about whether or not you're okay. I mean it, Monah. I need you to do this for both our sakes."

Tears gathered in her eyes as he spoke. He lowered his head and kissed the tip of her nose. A few feet away, Casey turned her back to give them privacy.

"What if we're wrong?" Monah whispered. "What if Ken didn't set the fires or kill Wayne Drolen and Charlotte Tait?"

He chuckled with relief. At least she wasn't arguing. "I'm pretty sure you and Casey can put your heads together and come up with another scenario."

"I bet we can." She laughed and rested her head against his shoulder, her arms tight around his waist. "Just be careful, okay? And you promise to let me know the minute you finish questioning Ken?"

"I promise." He pressed a quick kiss to her lips then led her back to her car. Once she and Casey were safely inside, he got in his own vehicle and headed down the lane. Ken met him halfway and rolled down his window.

"You're a little late, probie. I'm gonna have to fire you for this," he called cheerfully.

Dirt and soot crusted his eyes and made him look like a raccoon. How could a guy who looked like that be guilty of arson and murder? Mike shook his head.

"I've got a lead on the fires. Can you meet me at the police station?" Instinctively, his hand moved to his sidearm. If Ken refused, he'd have to arrest him and drag him in for questioning.

Ken's eyes narrowed as he followed the movement. "Is there a problem, Detective?" His voice was deceptively calm.

Mike shrugged. "I hope not."

After a moment's hesitation, Ken nodded. "Okay. I'll follow you."

Mike put up his window, turned the car around, and pulled onto the highway. Ken trailed behind.

Inside the station, the air buzzed with normal activity. Neither Ken nor Mike said a word as they wound their way to Mike's office and closed the door.

"What's this about, Mike?" Ken said, flopping into a chair. "I'd kinda like to get home and shower off."

Eyeing his friend, Mike circled the desk and eased into his chair. *How could you?* thrummed through his brain. "Where were you this morning, Ken?"

Ken rested both elbows on the desk and pressed his index fingers to his lips. His gaze as he stared at Mike was steady, measuring. For several moments, neither of them spoke. Finally, he leaned back in the chair and blew out a sigh. "How did you know?"

"About the fires? Someone saw you."

"By someone, you mean Monah?"

Mike's heart leaped in fear. "What difference does it make?"

Ken half laughed and rubbed a dirty hand over his face. "Not much."

At least he wasn't denying his crimes. That would have made his betrayal so much worse. Mike took out a sheet of paper and a pen and shoved them across to him. "I'm going to need you to give me a statement." The words came out cold, hard. . .exactly the way Mike felt.

Ken didn't move. "For what it's worth, I never meant to hurt anybody. It was all about the money and saving the fire department."

"Tell that to Wayne Drolen's widow," Mike snapped.

"What?" Ken sat up, and Mike tensed. "I didn't have anything to do with that."

"You're a two-faced liar," Mike said, anger coiling in his gut. "You expect me to believe a word that comes out of your mouth?"

Ken's face flushed, and he gripped the arms of his chair. "Now listen here, Brockman—"

The scanner crackled, cutting off what he'd been about to say.

"Attention all volunteer firefighters in the vicinity of Post Oak and Elm, there's another fire. I repeat, a fire on the corner of Post Oak and Elm."

CHAPTER ♜♜♜ TWENTY-NINE

For several seconds, the men could only sit and listen. Another fire? How was that possible? Ken had been here with him and, before that, the boathouse. It was too much of a coincidence to think this fire was legitimately an accident, but if it was arson, who was responsible?

The scanner crackled again. "Be advised—possible victims inside. Neighbors have reported vehicles in the driveway. Ambulance crews have been dispatched to 7204 Post Oak Drive. ETA—six minutes."

Ken jumped to his feet.

Mike followed. "Whoa. Where do you think you're going?"

"To the fire." He jabbed his thumb toward the door. "They're going to need help." He took a step in that direction.

Grabbing his arm, Mike jerked him around. "In case you haven't figured it out, you're under arrest for the murders of Charlotte Tait and Wayne Drolen."

Ken's mouth dropped open, and he yanked his arm free. "Are you kidding me?" he shouted, the muscles in his neck bulging. "I was with Lois Frederick when Drolen was killed."

"Save it, Ken."

He slapped his palm flat against the desk. "Ask her!"

Mike strode to the door and threw it open. "Lois!" Several

heads spun in his direction, but he was too angry to care. "Can you come in here, please?"

She scurried to them, her eyes wide. "Sir?"

"Where were you the day Wayne Drolen died?"

"Excuse me?"

"Fourth of July. The fund-raiser. Do you remember where you were when Drolen was killed?"

"I was w–with Ken."

Ken whirled to him. "See?"

"The whole time?" Mike continued.

"Most of it. At least three hours."

"Thanks, Lois." She stared, her mouth agape as Mike soundly closed the door. He crossed back to the desk and sat down.

"Mike—"

He shook his head. "It makes no difference. You're still a criminal, and I'm locking you up."

"Fine. Jail me *after* we put out the fire. I'll give you a statement, make a complete confession, whatever." He waved his hand. "In the meantime, we've got a possible victim and no firemen. They're still out at the boathouse." He pounded the desk. "Think, Mike! You know I'm right. We're wasting time standing here arguing!"

Jerking out of his chair, Mike sent it crashing against the wall. "You expect me to let you walk around free? How can I be sure you won't run?"

Anger pinched the corners of Ken's mouth. "You know me better than that."

"I thought I did."

Silence fell as the men stared at one another.

"So you're ticked, is that it? You're gonna let a woman die in order to soothe your pride?"

A deep chill spread over Mike's frame. "How do you know the victim is a woman?" he asked, his voice deadly low.

Ken shook his head. "7204 Post Oak Drive. Don't you recognize it?"

Mike frowned.

"That's Wayne and Dena Drolen's place."

The information hit Mike like a kick in the gut. "You've got to be kidding."

Suddenly, it seemed as though all of Ken's anger whooshed out and left him deflated. His shoulders slumped and he lifted pleading eyes. "She's in trouble, Mike. You could put me in a cell and try to help her yourself, but you're no fireman. Are you willing to risk Dena Drolen's life?"

Indecision ripped through Mike's insides. "The volunteers might get there in time to help." His voice sounded as uncertain as he felt.

"It'll take them twenty minutes, minimum. We're five minutes away." Ken waited in silence. "C'mon, buddy," he said softly. "It's the right thing to do, and you know it."

Mike grabbed his keys. "Fine, let's go. Might as well see if I can save a life since I probably won't be able to save my job after this."

Tires squealing, they drove the five minutes to Dena Drolen's house and made it in four. Several people lined the yard, many of them pointing as flames licked from the upper-story windows.

"Which way?" Mike panted as he leaped from the car and Ken from the fire truck. Together they jogged up the driveway.

Ken pointed toward the garage. "We'll go in the back. Too much heat in the front."

They didn't even pause at the heavy electric door, but circled to the side. It was locked.

"Stand back." Mike braced himself then broke out the window with his elbow. Reaching inside, he turned the bolt and rushed inside the garage.

"Wait!" Ken shouted. "Test the knob!"

His words brought Mike up short. He stepped aside and let Ken check the door leading into the house for heat. "Are those suitcases?" Mike said, stumbling against something stacked beside the door.

Ken spared a quick glance. "Looks like it. It's all clear." He pushed open the door. A cloud of smoke billowed out. Ducking his head through, he shouted, "Dena! Can you hear me?" He looked over his shoulder at Mike. "I'll go first. Stay behind me. If the smoke starts to sting your eyes or if you can't breathe, drop to your hands and knees and crawl. Do *not* go upstairs by yourself. It's not safe to split up. Got it?"

"Got it."

He followed as Ken cautiously entered the house. They called for Dena again and again, but with noise from the fire and the screaming of the smoke detectors, Mike doubted she'd hear.

Smoke filled the kitchen, and though the power had gone out, the heat had yet to penetrate.

"Anything?" Ken rasped.

Mike circled the table and peeked underneath. "Nothing." His eyes started to water. He wiped his sleeve across them and joined Ken by the entrance to the living room. "Let's go."

Ken grasped his shoulder. "Stay close."

His throat thick, Mike could only nod. Despite everything he now knew, Ken was still his friend.

The smoke was noticeably denser inside the living room. Ken bent at the waist and hollered for Dena, his hands cupped around his mouth. Mike did the same.

"Dena, can you hear me?"

Suddenly, Mike caught a glimpse of a pale limb jutting out from the base of the stairs. He grabbed Ken's arm and pointed then rushed to her.

A small bag and a cosmetic case lay scattered around her. Mike pushed them aside and lifted her easily into his arms.

"Follow me," Ken shouted.

Outside, sirens joined the crescendo rising from the alarms. *Thank God,* Mike thought. Dena was going to need medical attention. Curving his upper body to shield her from the heat and smoke, he stumbled after Ken the way they'd come in.

"This way," Ken said, coughing as they broke free of the garage.

The ambulance crew met them halfway across the yard. One of them took Dena from Mike, and the other grabbed his arm.

"You okay?"

Mike nodded, a deep cough rattling past his throat.

Ken gestured toward the volunteer firefighters who had just arrived and were frantically uncoiling the fire hoses. "I've gotta go help."

Though his voice was desperate, he waited for Mike to give the okay before running off to join them.

His heart heavy, Mike watched him go. The arsons, the lies—those were not done by the Ken he knew. The Ken he knew was fighting to save a family's home. He was battling alongside his men, protecting them, protecting his community.

The Ken he knew was not a murderer, and that meant Mike's job was far from over.

CHAPTER   THIRTY

The distant sound of sirens made Monah want to go search for Mike. She grabbed her office chair and held on, fighting a swell of fear for the man she loved. He had asked her to stay, and she would.

Casey patted her back. "Come on. Let's focus on our research." She tapped the laptop sitting on the desk. "Working might be the only thing that gets you through all this waiting."

Monah closed her eyes and said a silent prayer for Mike's safety. Then she put her fingers on the keyboard. "What was I looking for?"

"We were going to start by learning more about monkshood."

"That's right." She typed the word into the search engine then groaned. "A hundred and ninety thousand results."

"No problem. We only need to look at a few. I just want to know a little more about what we're dealing with."

Monah clicked on the first result listed. "Also known as aconite and wolfsbane." She scanned, reading aloud some of the main items. "Belongs to the buttercup family. Good grief. There's over 250 species."

"Yeah, but look at that one." Casey tapped the screen. "Click on Northern Blue Monkshood, also known as *Aconitum noveboracense*. Since it's a northern variety, it might be the one we're looking for. I wish we'd gotten that box from Sandy so we'd know the exact kind."

A thought flashed through Monah's mind. "Oh, wait."

"What?" Casey leaned forward and peered into her face.

"Hang on." Monah closed her eyes and, sticking her fingers behind her glasses, rubbed her lids. Where had she seen that name before? It sounded so familiar.

Casey grabbed her wrist and pulled her hand away. "Whaaat?"

"I've seen that *Aconitum* word before."

"Really? Where?"

Monah made a face. "That's what I'm trying to remember if you'd give me a minute."

Casey zipped her finger and thumb across her lips, laced her fingers in her lap, and looked up toward the ceiling. Monah shook her head and forced herself to concentrate.

What was it Casey said that rang the bell in her head? They should have gotten Sandy's box.

"That's it!"

"What's it? Come on. Spill it." Her hands fluttered.

Monah grabbed Casey's fingers. "A box with the word *Aconitum noveboracense*, or however you say that."

"What about it?"

All of Casey's questions were making her lose focus. She stood and walked away from the desk. "You remember me complaining about always getting Dena Drolen's mail?"

"Yeah, something about your addresses being similar. Drove you crazy."

"Right." Monah moved to the window and tried to visualize what she remembered. "It's stopped now, but for about three months or more, I'd get Dena's mail and she would come here to pick it up. Early on, a small box arrived for her. I remember it mainly because of the strange name stamped on top."

Casey joined her at the window. "*Aconitum nove*—whatever."

"Yeah, but it wasn't from any garden club, if I remember right. I think it had the name of some catalog company on the label."

Casey's mouth dropped open. "You're not saying you think she killed her husband?"

Monah shivered. "You never know. But how does Miss Tait fit into the picture? I can't think of any reason Dena would kill her."

"But if she had access to your water bottles—" Casey's eyes grew wide, and she stared at Monah. "Did Mike ever get the results back of the tests they ran?"

Monah frowned. "Not that he's mentioned. What? You think *she* put poison in the water? I can't believe I ever gave her time to get that done."

Casey grasped her hand. "What if she poisoned the water at home and switched a bottle out while you were getting her mail? And what if Miss Tait wasn't her intended victim?"

A chill started in Monah's scalp and raced down her spine. A tremor followed the same course but didn't stop until it reached her ankles. She wobbled to the desk and dropped onto the chair. "You think she wanted me dead? Why?"

"Because you witnessed her receiving the poison."

"So, no one from the garden club deliberately sent seeds to everybody to cover up their crime." Monah tried to swallow, but no moisture remained in her mouth. She rubbed her arms. "Is it cold in here to you?"

She glanced around the office and pulled out a drawer, looking for her sweater. Maybe it was at the counter. She got up to check. A siren grabbed her attention before she made it to the door. She peered out the window. An ambulance rushed by. Another shiver rolled down Monah as she thought of Mike getting hurt. She ran for her purse.

"I can't stay here, Case. I gotta see if Mike's okay."

"Call him."

Monah reached for her phone then remembered Casey had put it in the console pocket. "My phone's in my car. I'll call him on the way to the hospital."

"But you were supposed to stay here."

"If that's him in that ambulance. . ." She couldn't finish.

Casey didn't hesitate but grabbed her own purse. "Let's go."

Monah couldn't get to the car fast enough. She hit the UNLOCK button and dove for the phone. Listening to it ring, she buckled in and started the car. Five. Six times. She snapped it closed.

"He's not answering." Her voice quivered.

"Maybe I should drive."

Rather than answer, Monah shoved the car in gear and chased after the ambulance. They arrived at the hospital just as the medics wheeled the gurney into the emergency room. She screeched to a stop and raced after them, Casey on her heels.

"Ma'am, you can't leave your car there." The scowl on the nurse's face made Monah slide to a stop.

Casey grabbed her arm. "Give me your keys. I'll move it."

Monah handed them over and ran for the gurney, ignoring the shout that she couldn't go beyond the doors. She caught up at the same time they pushed the individual into a room.

Standing in the doorway, gaping at a filthy face, Monah's mind bounced between relief and shock. As far as she knew, Mike was still fine. But what had happened to Dena Drolen?

~

Working feverishly, the volunteer firefighters quickly beat down the flames consuming Dena's house. Maybe she wouldn't lose everything. Most of the damage seemed to be contained upstairs.

Mike watched as the firemen trudged through the waterlogged house into the yard. No doubt they were exhausted. Two fires in one day.

Behind them came Ken, his face tired and dirty. He pointed, directing men to hot spots he wanted them to keep an eye on. "Put a little more water on the roof," he ordered, "and I want two of you to check the attic for smolders."

Mike crossed the muddied yard to him. "You all right?"

Ken's shoulders slumped. He swallowed hard and turned his back to his men. "I'm fine. I just hate. . . A lot of them looked up to me, ya know? I let them down."

A surge of compassion swelled inside Mike's chest, replacing the anger he'd felt earlier. This was not going to be easy for either of them. "I know."

His eyes dark and filled with pain, Ken looked at Mike. "For just a second, I was tempted to stay in there. You know. Just not come out."

"That isn't the answer. It's the coward's way, and you're no coward." He clasped Ken's shoulder.

Tears flooded Ken's eyes. "Thanks. I was afraid you'd think the worst after—" He broke off and ducked his head.

Mike hesitated. *Give me the words, Lord*, he prayed silently. He took a deep breath. "You made a mistake, Ken. That you're sorry for what you did is not enough. Now it's time to face the consequences." He gave Ken's shoulder a squeeze, urging him without words to look up, which he did. "But it's going to mean a lot to the men if you come forward on your own. Especially after they hear why you did what you did."

Hope flared in Ken's eyes. "Mike. . .I. . .thanks." He bobbed his head just once, but it communicated everything he wanted to say.

Mike turned back to the house where the fire now seemed completely under control. Single file, the firemen had begun carrying items out of the house and depositing them in the yard. Mike glanced at Ken. "Any idea what happened in there?"

He shook his head. "It's strange. Most of the heat seemed to originate in the upstairs bedroom. From what I could tell, the hottest point was the fireplace. But why would Dena have a fire in the middle of summer?"

It didn't make sense, but not much of what had been happening in Pine Mills lately did. Mike shrugged and turned his attention to a couple of volunteers who were lugging two large, heavily soaked suitcases out of the garage. So, it was luggage he tripped over earlier.

The knowledge added more questions to the ones piling up inside Mike's head. Just where had Dena been going?

CHAPTER ⚏ THIRTY-ONE

Monah paced the hall outside Dena's room, waiting for the doctors to come out. How Casey managed to talk the nurse into letting them stay, she didn't know, but praise God, she did. Now, if someone would just tell them what had happened. They'd been here for over an hour. How much longer? And where was Mike? Did he know Dena was here?

He still hadn't answered his cell phone. Dismissing her fears for his safety became more and more difficult. Maybe she should try again.

His phone didn't get a chance to ring once. A doctor pushed through the emergency room doors. She slapped the phone closed. "Doctor, wait." She rushed to his side. "What's wrong with Dena? Will she be okay?"

"Are you a member of her family?"

Rats! "No. We're friends."

The doctor shook his head. "Then I can't discuss her condition with you."

He turned away. Monah stepped in front of him. "Doctor." She put on her most persuasive face. She didn't have to fake the emotion. "Dena's husband just died. I was with her when it happened. I just want to help if I can."

The doctor examined her face and heaved a deep sigh. He

looked around then led her further down the hall.

"Look, I shouldn't do this, but I can't see how it'll hurt to tell you a little. Especially if you're good friends." He glanced each direction. "One of the first things we look for in a fire victim is cyanide poisoning. . ."

Fire victim? She didn't have time to think. The doctor kept talking.

". . .so she's on 100 percent oxygen for now. It doesn't look like too severe a case. Just enough to cause weakness and dizziness. Might even have made her pass out, which would explain why they found her at the bottom of the stairs. She's got a concussion. We'll keep an eye on her for a while."

Monah frowned and scratched the back of her head. "She's fighting cyanide poisoning?"

"Right. Look, I've said too much already. I gotta go. They're waiting for me in another room."

Casey appeared at her side. "What'd he say?"

Monah filled her in as best she could then flipped open her cell phone. "I gotta find Mike. He needs to know about Dena."

She said a prayer and punched in his number. "Please, Lord. Let him answer." Three. Four.

"Hello." Mike's voice sounded raspy and a little terse.

"Mike! Where have you been? I've been trying to get you forever. Are you okay?"

"I'm fine. You okay?"

He sounded tired. "Good. Um, I'm at the hospital. Did you know Dena Drolen's been in a fire? She's—"

"Monah! I told you to stay at the library."

She smiled at the concern in his tone. "I heard a siren and saw an ambulance go by. You hadn't called, so I thought it might be you and chased it to the hospital."

His sigh was audible over the phone. "You realize how dangerous that was, right?"

"Never mind about that. Did you hear what I said about Dena being here?"

Long silence. "Yes. I'm at her house right now."

"Oh." The poor guy needed to rest. But she knew him well enough to know he wouldn't rest until the killer was caught. "Mike, I need to tell you something. The doctor said Dena had cyanide poisoning. Kinda surprised me since Casey and I thought it'd be monkshood poisoning."

"Why would you think that?"

There was no easy way to say this. "We think she's the one who poisoned Miss Tait and Wayne."

More silence. He must be trying to digest the news. "How did you two come to that conclusion?"

She explained about the mail mix-up and receiving the box containing the monkshood. "And that's not all of it, Mike."

"That's quite a bit all by itself. What else could there be?"

She took a breath, the news still hard to swallow. "We don't think Miss Tait was the target. We think she intended to poison me."

~

After warning Monah to be careful, Mike said good-bye and hung up his phone. He sought out Ken and found him stowing gear on the fire truck.

He jerked his thumb toward the house. "How long before we can go in?"

Ken swung his gaze to the house and back. "Shouldn't be long. Why?"

Mike relayed the information Monah had given him and gestured to the house. "I need to know how that fire started,

Ken. Can you help?"

Ken hesitated a moment then gave a quick nod. "Cyanide poisoning, you say?" he said as they picked their way through the mess strewed in the garage and into the kitchen. Water dripped from the windows and cabinets, and soot left dark spirals on the ceiling.

"Yeah. What do you know about that?"

Ken shrugged. "It's actually not that unusual in victims of a fire. It's a by-product of burning wool, which means carpet, furniture, even clothing can cause injury."

Mike glanced around the damaged room. Dena's floors were hardwood. Though there was plenty of smoke and water damage, the curtains were untouched by flames. Upstairs, conditions were much the same.

"So burning wool causes cyanide poisoning?" He squatted next to the fireplace, where the most significant damage had occurred. Reaching inside the firebox, he felt around until he found the lever for the flue. It was closed.

Ken squatted next to him. "Yeah, but if you're thinking what I'm thinking, that would be a little difficult, since all her floors are oak."

Mike nodded. "Ken, why would a woman who just lost her husband pack her bags and then burn something in her fireplace with the flue closed?"

Ken's brows rose.

"Yeah, doesn't make sense." Mike pulled a plastic bag from his pocket. Working carefully, he scooped up some of the ash scattered about the hearth and secured the bag. "Let's go," he said, rising to his feet. "I want to get this to the lab, and then we need to get to the hospital."

CHAPTER ⛩ THIRTY-TWO

Monah chewed on her thumbnail until Casey slapped her hand.

"I can't help it. I'm dying to know something, Case." She scooted low in her chair and hid her mouth behind her hand. "I'm gonna sneak in there. I've gotta know what's going on."

Casey grabbed her arm. "You can't go in. The nurses are watching." At that, she cast a glance toward said nurses and lowered her voice. "Besides, they told you she'd be fine. Don't forget, she wanted you dead."

"We don't know that for sure. That's just supposition on our part." Tension pushed Monah up in the chair. She made a fist. "Come on, Case. Something inside me feels the need to check on her. I gotta go."

Casey worried her bottom lip with her teeth. Finally, she nodded. "Okay. I'll do what I can to distract the nurses."

Monah squeezed her hand. "Thanks. I'll go to the water fountain and pretend to get a drink. When I think they're not looking, I'll make a break for it."

Water trickled from the fountain for what seemed like an hour. A nurse glanced sharply her way. Monah dipped her head and let the cool stream dribble over her chin. Still, the woman stared. She could drown before the woman turned away. Why didn't she go on about her work?

Suddenly, a sobbing woman emerged from a room on the other side of the counter. The nurse rushed to her aid. Monah dashed from sight. Standing outside Dena's door, she panted to catch her breath and rubbed her sleeve across her chin. That was too close—

She broke off in midthought. A drop of water dangled from the tip of her finger then splashed to the floor.

The water.

She gave Dena two bottles of water at the fund-raiser, one for her and one for Wayne. The day at the library, when she accused Monah of murdering Wayne, Dena claimed she never drank hers, but Monah was almost certain she'd seen her take a swallow. She risked a peek around the corner. The nurse hovered alongside the woman from the next room.

Casey's eyes were as big as saucers. *What are you doing?* she mouthed.

Monah gestured toward Dena's room and ducked back around the corner. Returning to ask Casey if she remembered seeing Dena drink was too risky. Who knew when the nurse might be distracted again?

She slipped into Dena's room without knocking. The bed was empty. A robe hanging from a hook brushed softly across her arm as she eased the door closed. Where could she be? She stepped toward the bathroom and came face-to-face with Dena.

"Y–you're awake," she stammered. "Great. I guess you're feeling better."

The corners of Dena's mouth twitched. "Yeah, better." She patted a loose strand of hair into place. "What are you doing here?"

She grasped for an answer. "I. . .wanted to check on you."

"Thank you. I'm fine. I'll talk to you later, okay?" She turned away.

Monah stared. Strange. "You're dressed." A hospital gown lay in a heap on the floor next to the bed. "They approved you to go home?"

Dena doubled over and grasped the IV stand.

Monah rushed to her side. "Are you all right?"

Dena growled and shoved her against the wall. Monah stumbled and landed in a sprawl on the chair. She looked up. Dena held the bottom of the IV stand in her face.

"Why did you have to come in here?" She shook the stand as she talked. "If you weren't so nosy, you wouldn't get into so much trouble."

"But I—"

"Shut up." Dena loosened the hand screw on the IV pole then slid the two sections apart. Letting the bottom drop, she wielded the top like a sword. "All I wanted to do was get rid of my cheating husband. Simple, right?" Tears formed. She brushed them away impatiently.

"Dena, I—"

"Don't say another word." The order came out through gritted teeth. "You and that stupid post office. I had it all planned out, right up until you started getting my mail. Then, when I knew you'd seen the box of seeds. . ."

"You meant that poisoned water for me instead of Miss Tait." The sentence came out as a statement. An evil laugh ripped from Dena's lips, and questions raced through Monah's mind.

Dena shook her head, an odd smile still on her face. "It wasn't the water, Monah. In fact, I blame you for Charlotte's death. If you hadn't given her your sweater, she'd still be alive."

"My sweater? But I thought—"

"That's just it—you didn't think." Her mouth in a snarl, Dena held the rough end of the pole closer to Monah's throat. "Oh, but I'd done my homework. I took your sweater home and soaked the sleeves with a mixture of monkshood and a solvent to make the poison absorb into the skin faster. Then I put your sweater back and poured acid on your air conditioner wiring to make sure it wouldn't shut off. And you had to ruin everything. . .again!"

Monah swallowed hard. Dena had lost her mind.

Dena took two deep breaths. "If only you'd put on that stupid sweater. But no, you made me go through the trouble of planting monkshood seeds under the counter and marking up your gardening books in order to make you look guilty." She wobbled then shook her head and righted herself, gripping the pole until her knuckles turned white. "But I'll take care of that mistake right now."

"Dena, wait."

Scowling, Dena shook her head. "I've waited long enough. With you gone, there'll be no witnesses."

She lifted the pole high.

In an instant, Monah decided she wouldn't just give up. She closed her eyes and lunged from the chair.

~

A crowd of people waited outside the elevator. Mike frowned. Where in the world were they all going? He'd never seen the hospital so busy.

He glanced at his watch. By now Ted could very well have the results he'd asked for. He tugged his phone from his pocket, but instead of punching in the numbers, he looked upward at the lighted display above the elevator doors. Something was pushing him up there.

The doors whooshed open. A soft bell chimed. He squeezed

in, but as several people punched the numbers to varying floors, he changed his mind and jumped off. "Sorry," he yelled amid a chorus of groans. Jogging now, he launched himself toward the stairs.

When he entered the hospital, an emergency room nurse had told him Dena had been moved to a private room on the fourth floor. Heat assailed him as he threw open the stairwell door. If he hurried, he should be able to beat the elevator easily.

He did more than hurry. An odd urgency pressed on his chest, moving him up the stairs two, sometimes three at a time. Bursting onto the fourth floor, he looked down the hall to his left and then to his right. Casey rushed over to him.

"Thank goodness you're here."

"Where is she?"

Her finger jutted toward the far end of the hall. "Down there."

"Wait here." He speared her with a firm glance. She nodded. Mike strode down the hall.

"Sir—"

Mike flashed his badge at the nurse, effectively silencing her. "Dena Drolen's room?"

"Four twenty-three," she stammered.

He replaced the badge in the breast pocket of his blazer. His steps slowed as he neared the door. From inside the room, voices drifted. One was definitely Monah's, and she sounded—

"Dena, wait."

Mike froze, his heart pounding.

"I've waited long enough. With you gone, there'll be no witnesses."

Almost without thinking, Mike withdrew his sidearm and kicked open the door. "Freeze, Dena!"

Dena hunched over a cowering Monah, half an IV stand

clasped in her hands. Her mouth dropped as she stared at him in bewilderment. Taking advantage of her surprise, Mike strode further into the room, the gun pointed steadily at her head.

"Drop the weapon and back away. Now!"

She flinched as he barked the order. Suddenly, her fingers went limp, and the stand clattered to the floor.

"Monah, you okay?" He spared a quick glance at her pale face. She scrambled to her feet. Sticking out his hand, he steered her safely behind him. "What happened?"

She clutched his shoulders, her small body trembling as she clung to him. "It was Dena. She murdered Miss Tait by accident. She meant to kill me because I saw the package of poison she ordered to kill Wayne."

Dena lifted her chin. "I almost got away with it. Some mystery writer you are. You never figured out that I used the sweater to poison Charlotte Tait instead of the water. If I hadn't told you—"

"Wrong, Dena," Mike said. "At this very moment, Ted Levy is analyzing the ashes we took from your fireplace. I'm pretty sure he's going to tell me they're laced with monkshood. Too bad you didn't realize that burning the sweater with the flue closed to hide the smoke would release a toxic amount of cyanide. Not enough to kill you but certainly enough to make you sick. Right, Dena?"

She merely scowled.

"So that's what happened? Dena tried to burn my sweater and got sick from the fumes?" Monah said.

The door burst open before he could answer.

"All right, everyone out. There are no visitors—" Seeing Mike holding Dena at gunpoint, the head nurse paused in midsentence and pressed her hand to her chest. "Oh my."

"Oh my is right," Casey said, peering over the nurse's shoulder at them. "Can somebody please tell me what is going on?"

Monah laughed and crossed to slip her arm around Casey's shoulders. "Okay, okay. I'll fill you in. But first," she looked back long enough to blow him a kiss, "let's step outside so Mike can read Dena her rights."

CHAPTER ♦♦♦ THIRTY-THREE

Everything in Mike's office reminded Monah of him, from the sturdy wooden shutters to the solid oak desk. She tucked her hands under her thighs and tried not to fidget while she waited for him to return from lockup.

"Well, that's over."

She stood as Mike entered. "So Dena made a statement?"

"Nope. She lawyered up. Don't know why. She blabbed to both of us what she'd done." He shoved a folder into his file cabinet.

Monah followed him around the desk, unable to take her eyes off her rescuer. "I think she planned to finish me off and then make a run for it."

"Yeah, well, she wouldn't have gotten far. We were already onto her." He slid the drawer closed and locked it. "You ready to go?"

Monah smiled. She was ready to go anywhere with him. "Where?"

He lifted his elbow for her to take and led the way out of the station. "I figure with all you've been through, you deserve a night out. How's dinner at Mason's sound?"

With a quick glance at her faded denims and wrinkled T-shirt, Monah made a face and shook her head. "I'm not dressed for that."

"Then how about a large pepperoni at Jake's?"

The way Mike's eyes sparkled, she knew that's what he'd wanted in the first place. "You know pizza is my favorite food, next to chocolate anyway."

He tweaked the end of her nose. "Pizza it is, with a chocolate malt on the side."

Monah laughed as she climbed into his car while he held the door. Instead of closing it, he stood smiling at her.

She finally frowned and wiped at her face. "What?"

"You were great today."

With a grin, Monah waved his words away. "I just slowed her escape until you showed up."

"And nearly got clobbered for your effort." He shut the door, walked to the other side, and climbed in. Leaning over, he kissed her cheek. "I'm glad you're okay."

He pulled out of the parking lot and then reached for her hand. Warmth radiated through her from his touch. She'd say the words tonight. When the right moment came, she'd tell him she loved him.

Ahead, the town's only stoplight turned yellow. Monah looked out the window and down the street. "This isn't the way to Jake's."

Mike didn't say a word. A minute later, he pulled to the curb and stopped. Still silent, he got out, opened her door, and helped her out. Keeping her hand in his, he led her down the sidewalk.

Monah tugged him to a stop. "Are you okay? What's wrong?"

He took a deep breath and slowly let it out. "I've had a lot on my mind lately."

"No doubt." She pressed her hand to his cheek. "But it's all over now. You caught Ken and stopped the arsons. You found out about a counterfeit operation and put the wheels in motion to shut it down. And Miss Tait and Wayne Drolen's murderer is now behind bars. Dena won't be able to hurt anyone again."

Mike dipped his head to look at her. "That's not what I was talking about."

Confused, Monah frowned. "Then what?"

He gently pushed her backward away from the curb. Anticipation growing, she looked into his eyes, soundlessly begging him to speak. He licked his lips.

"I need your help with something."

She nodded quickly "Anything."

He put his hands on her shoulders, paused, then turned her completely around until she faced a store window. "What do you think of that gold one in the middle—the one with the emeralds?"

Monah gulped in an effort to keep from crying. No longer did it matter what people thought of her. Mike accepted her for who she was. She sniffled.

"Hey." He leaned down and rested his cheek against hers. "Don't cry. I wanted this to be a happy thing." He turned her around then moved his hands to her cheeks and wiped her eyes with his thumbs. "I love you, Monah. I want to take care of you, spend every free moment with you." He smiled. "I'm hoping you'll agree to be my wife."

"Your wife?"

"Yeah." He dropped his hands to his sides. "I thought it might be the only way to get you to stay put when I tell you to."

Her mouth fell open, and she whacked him on the chest. Mike burst into laughter and pulled her into his arms. He leaned down and kissed her until they both nearly gasped for air.

A strand of hair blew across her face. Mike brushed it back into place. "So? Think you can handle life with an officer of the law?"

She grinned. "Are you kidding? I'll be living with ready-made ideas for my Brandy Purcell books."

A smile formed as he shook his head and put his hand over his heart. "I feel so used."

Placing her hand over his, Monah leaned closer. "I promise to make it up to you."

He leaned down until his face was mere inches from hers. "Deal." And he sealed it with a kiss. Before she could even enjoy the moment, Mike moved away. "You never answered me. Will you be happy with that diamond and emerald ring?"

Monah followed the direction he pointed. She stared at the ring in the middle until tears blurred her vision. "It's beautiful."

"Good. I've had my eye on that for a while now."

Wiping her eyes, Monah smiled. "Really?"

"Yeah, really." He took her hand. "We'll come back in the morning when it's open and have it fitted."

A cool breeze whipped up her hair again. She rubbed her arms. "Let's go. It's got to be warmer in Jake's."

"Here"—he started tugging off his sport jacket—"put this on."

Monah rubbed the cloth between her thumb and fingers. "Feels like wool."

He frowned. "It is."

The beginning of a smile pricked Monah's lips. She tilted her head and looked up at him. "In that case. . ."

His lips twitched in response. "Yeah?"

"In that case," she said, snuggling under his arm, "I think I'd rather be cold. They didn't come up with the saying 'died in the wool' for nothing, you know."

Mike's laughter bounced off the building. "It's 'dyed-in-the-wool,' as in 'trustworthy' or 'stalwart.' "

She shook her head. "Tell that to Miss Tait."

Still laughing, his arms encircled her waist. "I love you, Monah Trenary. I'm going to enjoy getting to know you better every day of my life."

She giggled. At last! The time was right. She peeked up into his face, a blush warming her cheeks. "I love you, too, Mike Brockman. I love you, too."

ELIZABETH LUDWIG is an award-winning author whose work has been featured on *Novel Journey*, the Christian Authors Network, and The Christian Pulse. She is an accomplished speaker and teacher and often attends conferences and seminars, where she lectures on editing for fiction writers, crafting effective novel proposals, and conducting successful editor/agent interviews. She is the owner and editor of the popular literary blog, *The Borrowed Book*. Along with her husband and two children, Elizabeth makes her home in the great state of Texas. To learn more about Elizabeth and her work, visit her at www.elizabethludwig.com.

JANELLE MOWERY lives in Texas with her husband and two sons, though a portion of her heart still resides in her birth state of Minnesota. Janelle began writing inspirational stories in 2001 and has since written several historical novels. Her first novel, *Where the Truth Lies*, was released in 2008. This was followed in 2010 by *The Christmas Chain*, part of a Christmas anthology titled *A Woodland Christmas*. Janelle's Colorado-themed Heartsong trilogy will release in 2011. When she isn't writing, her interests include reading, enjoying nature, and visiting historical sites. To learn more, visit her Web site at www.janellemowery.com.

You may correspond with these authors by writing:
Elizabeth Ludwig and Janelle Mowery
Author Relations
PO Box 721
Uhrichsville, OH 44683

Other
HOMETOWN MYSTERIES
from Barbour Publishing

Nursing a Grudge

Missing Mabel

Advent of a Mystery

Nipped in the Bud

May Cooler Heads Prevail

The Camera Never Lies

 Burying the Hatchet

Blown Away